CALEB'S TALE

by

Frank G Davis

This is the Second Edition with updated title.

First Printing Edition, 2022, under title: The Book of Caleb

Publisher **Authors Wild** Paperback ISBN: 978-1-954253-54-4

<u>DEDICATION</u>

This book is dedicated to the Inklings Writer's Group which meets on the first and third Thursday of each month at the Vista Grande Library in Casa Grande, Arizona.

The comments, criticisms and encouragement by the members of Inklings played a huge part in leading me to become a published author. Thanks to all of the Inklings members. I couldn't have done it without you!

INTRODUCTION

My name is Caleb Brown. What I'm about to tell you is difficult to believe. Perhaps, some of you will choose not to believe. Even I had a hard time accepting what happened to me so I can understand those who are skeptical. If you don't believe in supernatural events or divine intervention, you might be wasting your time to read any further. If you're curious and willing to listen to my story, you might believe or at least be entertained in my life after death.

I have a twin brother; his name is Joshua. We were, and still are, exceptionally close. We grew up in the south and our papa, Moses, was the pastor of a local church in a small community. He was a very big man and Joshua and I grew to be even bigger, a little over six feet, six inches. Joshua and I were inseparable as we matured from childhood to becoming adults. Our mama, Gloria, (Papa always called her Glorious) dressed us in identical clothes. It was always easier to buy two of everything then to have to decide over different outfits.

After high school we decided to join the Marines, just like Papa had done so many years ago. He always said being a Marine and going to war was the Lord's way of testing your beliefs. He served two tours in Vietnam and became a pastor after he was discharged.

Joshua and I were in the same Recon Company and served two tours in Afghanistan. We were eight days away from the end of our second tour when I was killed by an IED. That is where this story begins.

As devout Southern Baptists our entire family believed in a life after death but not exactly the existence that happened to me. Never in my wildest dreams did I ever think I would exist by being bonded to my twin brother. It was as much a shock to Joshua as to me.

CHAPTER 1

The Awaking—Joshua

When Caleb was killed, I died with him. Actually, I was mostly dead, not completely dead. I was on the other side of Kabul when he was killed by the IED. My squad and I had just finished mopping up a Taliban terrorist group. My assistant leader was questioning one of the Taliban survivors using one of the locals as an interpreter. I was listening intently to his answers. I spoke passable Pashto but nobody knew that. I wanted to see if our interpreter was giving us the real translations. One minute I was standing up listening, the next I was on the ground very close to death. It was like someone had flipped a switch from on to off.

When I regained consciousness, I was in a hospital with tubes, IVs and monitors attached to every square inch of my body, including my head. Later, much later, like almost a month later, I found out I was back in the States, fighting for my life and not doing a very good job of it.

I was in and out of being conscious for at least a week; it was hard to keep track of time. Eventually, I had a few lucid moments and they weren't very pretty. I remembered being blown up by the IED and feeling the intense pain of my body being ripped into a million tiny pieces. The next time I was listening to a Taliban captive trying to lie his way out of our control, "I'm not Taliban, you have made a terrible mistake, you have to lis…" then blackness again.

They kept me heavily sedated while I fought to regain…regain what? Eventually, I was able to stay awake for an hour or so before drifting off. I remember listening to my medical team talk about me, "This is so weird. According to the records it says he just passed out for no reason. He wasn't shot or hit by any debris. He just fell down and almost died. He didn't have a heart attack or stroke, not even a bruise on his body. What could have caused this?"

On other days, it was totally different, "What could have caused all this bruising. His entire body is swollen and his pain level is off the charts. The pain meds don't seem to have any effect on him."

Some of the less compassionate med team personnel started referring to me as the 'yoyo,' due to the way my symptoms kept changing back and forth so quickly.

Another month passed and I finally improved to remaining conscious for a much longer period of time. The yoyoing of physical injuries went away completely but a different type of yoyoing made itself known. On one day, I knew I was Joshua. On other days I was just as sure I was Caleb.

That's when they brought the psychiatrists in. They made it official, I was diagnosed as Looney Tunes. That was what I overheard one of the doctors who handled nut-cases say, "He's schizophrenic with a multi-personality disorder, Looney Tunes for sure."

They pumped me full of psycho-meds and shipped me off to a VA hospital to spend the rest of my life as a zombie. Also known as 'The Living Dead.'

A Man's Gotta Know His Limitations—Caleb

Slowly, very slowly, I began to realize what had happened to me. Or maybe I was just making it up as I went along. It was something like this: All human beings are born with a soul. It's what make each of us unique, even identical twins and triplets have different souls. They may be very similar but they aren't identical. Souls aren't made of flesh and blood, they are spirits and they are immortal. All this our papa taught Joshua and me when we were little children. I never thought much about it after I became an adult. While Joshua was zoned out on drugs, I had a lot of time to think. In fact that was all I could do. I seemed to be connected to Joshua but thank heavens his meds had no effect on me and apparently, I had little or no effect on him.

It seemed to me, we were now somehow bonded together. We had been very close when we were both alive. We literally did everything together. Even our thought patterns were nearly the same. How could I possibly know that? I submit as evidence the fact that we often, very often, began speaking at the same time and would speak in unison as if we were simultaneously reading a script or a page from a book. It was also routinely noted by our friends, one of us would begin a sentence and the other would finish it as if we were expressing the same thought.

When I was killed, I believe that bond continued. Except now I didn't have any body parts. I couldn't speak, hear or see, except that wasn't exactly true. I was able to hear whatever Joshua could hear. No, that's not accurate either. When Joshua was sleeping or unconscious from the meds, I could still hear the people in the room speaking. When he was awake, I could see through his eyes but for some reason, I couldn't speak through him. Are you confused yet? I was; I still am.

The bottom line of all this is I believe our spirits are bonded together. I'm not sure if it will last forever or only a few days but we are bonded now. That's what's important to me.

Another thing that's important to me is to get Joshua off those damn meds. I know in my heart (actually, I don't have a heart. Consider it a figure of speech) Joshua will return to normal if I can get him off the drugs. I need to find a way to make that happen.

I didn't have long to wait. "Wake up *hombre*. It's time for your *pildoras*." Joshua blinked a few times and finally focused on the short Hispanic man in a white smock carrying a little white cup. I was seeing the orderly through Joshua's eyes as he ordered, "Open wide."

I was taken by surprise, but as I sensed Joshua beginning to open his mouth I screamed *NO! Don't take the pills. They're poisoning you!* I screamed it with all my might but then remembered I didn't have a mouth or a voice. It was a waste of time. Except maybe it wasn't.

Josh quickly closed his mouth and turned his head around as if searching for someone.

The orderly had begun to pour the cup of pills into Joshua's mouth but ended up spilling them when my brother closed his mouth and turned his head. Several of the pills rolled down the front of his gown and onto the floor.

"*Ay pendejo*, look what you did, fool. The hell with you. You can do without your meds. I hope you suffer." He turned and quickly stormed out of the room as my brother kept searching.

In a weak, scratchy voice I heard him softly say, "Caleb?"

I answered back by thinking as if I were having a conversation, *I'm here, bro. I'm right here.*

I wasn't sure I'd gotten through to him again. He closed his eyes and laid back on the bed and began to drift back to sleep. Then I sensed his voice again, even weaker this time, *Thank God.* For the first time since I died, I felt joy again. If I had a mouth, I would have been grinning like a Cheshire cat.

While my brother slept, I began making plans on how to escape this nut house. Spirits don't sleep. At least I didn't sleep. Which was okay since I didn't get tired. It was like I was outside time. When something was going on I was fully conscious of what it was in real time. When everybody else was sleeping, it was like somebody hit the fast-forward button and time flew by until I needed to be conscious again. I hope that makes sense.

It was the middle of the night when I received a visitor. I was somewhere…else. I wasn't sure exactly where. It was a sunny spring day with a bright blue sky, laced with puffy white clouds and birds singing in the nearby trees. Colorful flowers were growing everywhere and their perfume fragrance scented the air. The ground was covered in perfectly manicured deep green grass. It reminded me of a movie set, too beautiful to be real or maybe it was all just my imagination.

I spotted a man walking briskly towards me. He was dressed in casual attire, a powder blue sweater over dark blue collared shirt, grey slacks and deck shoes. I was pleasantly surprised I had a body; I was dressed in the Marine battle gear I was wearing before the IED event. This was getting truly bizarre. I was beginning to freak out and dropped my weapon to the ready position and said in my most authoritative voice, "That's close enough, sir. Stop right there and raise your hands."

"Stand at ease, Sergeant," said the man. "I'm here to deliver a message to you."

I clicked off the safety and brought up my weapon pointing at his center of mass. "Please identify yourself, sir."

The man's expression changed. He was no longer smiling. In the blink of an eye, I was back in the war zone in Kabul pointing my weapon at my superior officer who was now also dressed in battle gear. There was all kind of gun fire going off in the distance, the sound of war was everywhere. "Lower your weapon, Sergeant, and stand easy," he repeated. It was Captain Collins, my company commander.

I lowered my weapon as I thought to myself, *What in the hell is going on?*

"You and your brother Joshua have been selected for a top-secret Mission. It may not seem like it now but this Mission is critical to plans from our commander in chief." He paused as a Russian tank operated by Taliban soldiers made its way around a building two blocks away and began opening fire on everyone in view. We ducked down behind a burned-out truck and he shouted over the sounds of the approaching tank. "In the next few minutes we are both going to die but our essence will continue. We're out of time. No matter what happens, stay with Joshua. Do you understand, Sergeant?"

"Yes sir, I understand," I shouted back as the tank came into view. Two Marines with RPGs opened up on the tank taking out the right tread immobilizing it which was followed by a second rocket that blew the tank's turret off the body, killing all of the Taliban crew.

The captain stood up and was instantly killed by machine gun fire. I crawled away, looking for additional cover. When I thought I was clear, I moved into a running crouch as quickly as I could. Three steps later, I stepped on the IED.

I was in shock. What in the hell just happened? It was bad enough to get blown up by an IED once. I didn't like it any better the second time. However, the message was clear: stay with Joshua, we are going to be needed for something very important. I wondered who my captain was referring to when he said the orders came from the commander in chief. Did he mean the President of the United States or was that just a metaphor for someone else?

If I had a head, I would have shaken it in disbelief. I thought when you died, everything came to a screeching stop. How could I have been so wrong.

We've Got to Get Out of this Place—Joshua

When I awoke the next morning, I felt almost alive for the first time in a very long time. I didn't hurt anywhere on my body and I no longer had a foggy brain. Then I remembered my dream, or was it a dream? I looked around the room and it was deserted except for the monitoring equipment. I hated the room, it was so…so sterile. It reminded me more of a prison cell than a hospital room. They even had hand and feet restraints to keep me from hurting myself or other people. Fortunately, they hadn't seen fit to restrain me, at least not yet.

"Caleb, are you hiding here somewhere?"

Before anyone could answer, my cheerful (NOT!) orderly burst into my room with his cup of happy pills. I remembered what happened last night and said in a firm voice, "Nothing for me today but thanks for offering."

"You're a funny guy but the doc says you got to take the pills every morning and night. Otherwise, you may go crazy again and start talking to creatures nobody can see but you."

"But I like talking to pretend people. They don't argue with me or try to dope me up so I don't know what I'm doing."

"I don't have time for your shit. You're going to take these pills right now. No more funny business or I bring in the gorillas to hold you down while I force feed you. If that don't work we turn you over and shove the pills up your *culo*. Maybe you like that better?"

"You're such a sweet talker. I bet your mother just loves to hear you talk like that, all sweet and lovey dovey."

The orderly stopped, frozen in place for a brief moment, then said, "Don't you talk about my mother, *Negro*. You go too far."

"Let's make a deal," I replied. "You stop giving me pills unless I start acting really weird and I won't say a word to you. It will make your day go better and mine too. Let's start today. No pills this morning or tonight and you check me the next morning to see if I've gone nuts again, deal?"

The orderly appeared lost in thought for a few moments then nodded his head, turned and left the room.

Well done, Josh.

"Caleb!?" I whispered. "Is that really you? Where are you?"

I can't tell you yet but I'm with you bro and I'm not going to leave you. We're going to get out of this hellhole really soon. Just hold on.

CHAPTER 2

Second Verse, Same as the First—Caleb

The rest of that day was uneventful, except for one very important thing; Joshua was getting stronger. Maybe most people couldn't see the difference but I could. I estimated he would be ready to leave this place in our rearview mirror in a day or two. He was far from being back to full strength but I thought he would be strong enough for a jail break. The orderly had been true to his word and didn't show up with pills at the time medications were dispensed. Instead, he brought in some real food for Joshua to eat. It was a welcome break from the nutrient IV line. I thought it might be sort of a peace offering. Joshua thanked him and the orderly smiled in return and commented that he thought he was looking stronger.

They turned off the lights at 2100 hours and Joshua was asleep a few minutes later. In a flash, I was back in wonderland, same bright sunny spring day, same fluffy clouds, same trees and flowers, etc., etc., etc. My commanding officer came walking towards me dressed in the same casual clothes. The only thing different was my outfit, no battle dress, no weapons, just stylish, navy blue workout clothes and some really cool Jordan runners.

"Let's try this again," said Captain Collins. "You have passed your initial test and are entitled to a few upgrades."

"Upgrades?" I was surprised. "Who are you? You aren't really Captain Collins, are you?"

"Very perceptive," he replied in a flat monotone voice. "I'm one of your training spirits. You were able to determine you're the spirit of Caleb Brown and were able to bond with your twin brother Joshua Brown. You demonstrated a mastery of mental telepathy with your brother in record time. As a result of these two accomplishments you will now be endowed with Spirit Sight which will permit you to view things in your immediate environment without being in direct contact with your brother. You will also be gifted the ability to travel anywhere in the world instantaneously and have limited contact with other spirits. Lastly, you will also be able to manipulate things, mostly small things at first but if you keep practicing you will be able to handle larger and more complex devices. I strongly recommend you use these new skills sparingly until you're sure of their limitations. Any questions?"

"Yeah, I have a lot of questions. First of all…"

"Sorry, our time is up for now."

I was back in Joshua's hospital room. I hoped I'd get used to these quick scene changes. They were really disorienting. However, I noticed I could now see everything much more clearly than before. The detail was a hundred times better. On a whim, I wondered if I could travel out of Joshua's room. *BAM!* Suddenly I was in the lobby of the hospital. This was so cool! But I needed to focus on our escape plan. *BAM!* I was back in Joshua's room again. I got started on the plan.

I wanted to get him out of the hospital as fast as possible. At the same time he needed to be strong enough to walk out of here and to the closest bus stop. Time to do some recon. I thought about bus stops close to the VA hospital. *BAM,* I was outside and staring at a bus stop sign. I need to clear something up. I still had no body; therefore I had no eyes. I have no idea how I was able to see but I could. I could also approximate turning my head and look back over my shoulder to see the hospital parking lot about a half block from the hospital (remember, I had no head to turn and no shoulder to look over but it felt to me that was exactly what I was doing).

The next step in the plan was to figure out how I was going to be able to get some cash to pay for our escape. We needed bus fare and money or credit cards to cover our food and probably a motel. I focused on the employee locker room. *BAM!* I was in a large co-ed locker room, one side for men and the other for women. Okay, I'm going to stop saying *BAM* when my sprit changes locations. Once or twice was all right but now it seems more like something you'd see in a Batman and Robin comic book.

In spite of my new skills, I needed Joshua. I could 'reach' into a locker and pull out a wallet or a purse, but he would have to carry them; sprits have no pockets. There was another issue, a much bigger and more important issue, I hadn't addressed; he wasn't aware I was a spirit. I had been putting him off but I had to come clean soon…but not just yet. I hope to confront him after we are safely out of the hospital and on our own.

Time for The Great Escape—Joshua

I awoke the next morning feeling even better than the day before. I vaguely remembered Ernesto (the orderly) bringing in a tray of food for breakfast while I was still dozing. I took one look at the tray and my stomach began to growl and my saliva glands kicked in. There was a slice of ham, two eggs scrambled hard with cheddar cheese, hash browns, whole wheat toast, coffee and orange juice. I thought to myself, *this can't be hospital food!* I dug in and forgot all about where he'd gotten the food. It smelled delicious and tasted heavenly.

I finished breakfast in record time and felt the need for a bathroom visit. A thought occurred to me, instead of ringing for Ernesto to assist me, I decided to see if my body still worked. I cautiously swung my legs over the side of the bed and very gradually began to stand up. To my great surprise, I was able to stand. I was a little wobbly and it seemed like it took forever to get to the bathroom, however I made it just in time to answer the call of nature.

On the way back to the bed, I felt even stronger and decided to skip the bed and sit in the easy chair to wait for Caleb. I used the remote to turn on the TV and watched the national news while I waited.

Good morning, Josh. How're you feeling, bro?

My brother's voice seemed to be coming from behind me, near the door to the hall. I started to turn around, but he said, *Please don't turn around, I look a mess. Just listen. Are you up to getting out of this cell block?*

"I sure am. I'm feeling surprisingly strong, not strong enough to leap a tall building in a single jump, but strong enough to mosey on out of here," I answered. "What's the plan?"

He went over the plan, step by step, answering all my questions and I could tell he was getting excited about being out of this place and on our own again.

He finished up the briefing and told me to rest and build up my strength. He suggested I get back in bed to look weaker than I was and schedule with Ernesto to have lunch and dinner a bit earlier if possible. We were leaving at 0300 hours.

CHAPTER 3

And Away We Go!—Caleb

I woke Joshua at 0230 hours. It was dark in the room; I'd turned off all the room lights and told him I'd go first and he would wait a few minutes then follow. The employee dressing room was a short walk down the hall to his right and I made sure the door was unlocked and opened a crack. I had transported inside the locker room and opened all the various lockers checking wallets and purses and clothes that would fit Josh.

Joshua pushed open the hall door and slipped inside. I had left only a few lights on, those that shined on the benches in front of open lockers. He quickly saw the extra tall clothes I had found, discarded his hospital gown and slipped on the clothes. They were a little small, however they would have to make do until we got out of town.

We 'borrowed' three credit cards from various wallets and took all the cash we could find. I had limited my search for cash to the doctors and was able to collect a little over a $1,000 from five different doctor's lockers, taking not more than $300 from any one doctor. They probably wouldn't even notice the money was missing. I also took a smart phone from one of the lockers and two ear buds. We'd use it to search the internet when needed and a number of other things.

I told Joshua to head out to the bus stop while I cleaned up. After he left, I closed all the locker doors at once and relocked them, closed and locked the door to the hall, checked to make sure Joshua had exited the hospital and relocked the main door.

I could 'see' Joshua waiting at the bus stop. Atlanta has a great bus system but late at night they only stopped once an hour at the hospital. Joshua kept looking for me. When I hadn't shown up when the bus stopped, he still climbed aboard like I had told him to do. He took a seat towards the back of the bus, looking worried. I transported to a seat just behind him. The overhead lights at the back of the bus were dim this time of night and I made them dimmer.

Hey, bro. We made it! I had to leave on the other side of the hospital. Security was looking for you. I flagged down the bus and they let me on. Sorry for the confusion.

He started to turn around. I said, *Eyes front. Pretend you don't know me until we get off the bus. There's an all-night diner about an hour from here. It's right on the way to the train station. We'll get off there.*

The Moment of Truth—Caleb

When our bus stopped near an all-night diner, I told Joshua to get off and I'd join him in the restaurant. There were only a handful of people in the place and he took a booth near the back wall to give us some privacy. I waited until he had ordered a piece of cherry pie a la mode and a cup of coffee. The waitress delivered it before I began.

We made it, Josh. We're free at last.

He put down his fork and looked for me. Of course there was nothing he could see. "Where are you, Caleb? Why are you hiding from me? Why can't I see you?"

Please just listen to me. This is going to be very hard to explain but let me try before you ask any questions. Please keep an open mind.

In a quiet voice, he replied, "What's going on, Caleb?"

Joshua, when you almost died in Afghanistan, it was because of me. When I stepped on the IED, I was killed instantly. That same instant you died too. I don't know why but I think it was because we were so close all of our lives. What I thought, you thought too. When you got sick, so did I and when I died in the explosion you died right along with me, even without an explosion. The only reason you survived was due to the corpsman who was on site with you and your squad. He revived you three times while they transported you to a field hospital where you died another time. Eventually, they were able to stabilize you.

I 'looked' closely at my brother before I continued. His eyes were closed and his hands were balled into tightly clenched fists.

I believe that every time they resuscitated you, my essence, my spirit, whatever you want to call it, was also brought back. My body was destroyed but my spirit survived. It took us almost a year before I figured out what was happening. The only reason I exist is because you exist. I am still connected to you. My spirit shares a part of your body. I can exist away from you but only for a little while. Without you, I will cease to exist.

I paused and I could see he was trembling. I didn't know what else to say. I needed to say something to calm him. Before I could think of what to say, he started babbling and his voice became louder and louder. "This can't be true. I'm losing my mind; the psychiatrists were right. I'm crazy, out of touch with reality, a real nut case. You can't be real, Caleb. You're dead and I'm crazy."

The few people in the diner started staring at him, and a man I assumed was the manager began walking slowly toward our booth.

"If you're real, you must be a ghost. GET OUT OF MY HEAD, GHOST!!! For God's sake let me be. Please leave me alone." Tears were streaming down his face as he screamed this over and over.

"Please, sir, I'm going to have to ask you to leave," said the manger in a firm voice. "You're scaring us. Don't worry about your bill, just leave."

Joshua jumped up and ran from the diner. I followed. It's funny how you notice unimportant things during times like this. The ice cream on the cherry pie was completely melted and was dripping off the plate onto the table as we left.

In as soothing a mental voice I could manage I kept asking him to stop running. That had no effect on him so I tried another approach. *You're getting very tired, so tired. You're not ready to be running away like this, your body isn't ready. You need to stop running, sit down and catch your breath. No one is following you. You're safe now. You just need to get some rest, you need to sleep, things will be better in the morning.*

To my surprise, he started to slow down and eventually stopped. He continued to sob as he bent over and put his hands on his knees. He had run into a park behind the diner and it was almost pitch black. I could see and hear the sound of him retching but he finally stood up and began to walk slowly through the park and I guided him to a bench. "So tired. So damn exhausted," he mumbled, barely audible. He laid down on the bench and fell into a deep sleep.

The Morning After—Joshua

I woke to the sound of birds chirping in the magnolia tree directly above me. I thought it was strange that a tree would be growing in my hospital room, not to mention there were several birds making all kinds of racket.

I was cold. I reached down to pull my blanket over me. Where the hell was my blanket? I rolled over and fell out of my bed…no wait! It wasn't my bed it was a park bench. What in the hell was I doing sleeping on a park bench?

The grass underneath me was damp with morning dew and I managed to get up and sit down on the bench. It all started to come back to me, very slowly and disjointed. I was hungry and I wished I had finished the cherry pie. It was my favorite, especially when it's covered in ice cream. Why did I run away from my brother? What did he say that made me run away from him? OH MY GOD! He's really dead and I'm really crazy.

I began rocking back and forth, strange sounds coming from my throat. Apparently, it was scaring the birds and they stopped their chirping. I had no idea how long I sat there but hunger finally forced me to stand up and head back toward the diner. Then I suddenly stopped. I remembered the manager had kicked me out for being a complete jerk.

I vaguely remembered Caleb had given me three credit cards and some cash before we escaped from the hospital. I reached into my pocket to see how much cash I had and froze. Caleb gave me the money! He also got me the clothes I was wearing (not quite large enough but okay for an escape). He unlocked all the doors so we could get out. How does a dead man do all that? The only logical answer I could come up with was, a dead man couldn't do all those things. Therefore, logic dictates Caleb isn't really dead. Thank you, Commander Spock. Could all the stuff he said to me be true? Was he really alive? Well, maybe 'alive' isn't quite the correct word. I remembered whoever was talking to me last night said my brother's body was dead but his spirit was alive. I was getting a headache just trying to figure all this out. My stomach began to cramp and strange sounds seemed to be coming from my belly.

I pulled the cash out of my pocket. *Wow! A thousand dollars.* "I'm rich," I said out loud. "I'm going to find a restaurant and have the biggest breakfast they can make."

There's an IHOP just a few blocks away. I know how much you like IHOP. Let's go there.

I let out a quick scream and almost fell down. "Damn! Caleb don't scare me like that. You are alive or at least your spirit is. I thought I was going crazy. I'm still not sure I'm not but for now I'm going to go with it. Lead on bro. I'm starving."

At the HOP—Caleb

"I'll have the Lumberjack Slam, two extra eggs scrambled hard with cheddar, coffee with hazel nut creamer and a glass of ice water, please," said Joshua to the server.

It was early and the restaurant was half full with customers. There was the buzz of conversation which was good cover for when I spoke to Josh. *Take out the smart phone I gave you last night and put one of the ear buds into your ear. When I 'speak' to you I don't really speak. I transfer my thoughts directly to your brain. Anyone seeing you speak to an invisible man will think you're on a phone call.*

"Kind of like telepathy?" Joshua asked.

Exactly like telepathy. Eventually, you're going to have to learn to do it as well. For now, the smart phone will be a good cover.

The server brought a huge platter of food and Joshua wasted no time digging into the chow. Since I was with my brother, I could share all of my brother's senses. The food smelled terrific and if I'd had a body, I'd be salivating just like Josh was. His taste buds were savoring the delicious taste of the food and I shared that as well. When he finished his meal, I had the sense of feeling full just like he did. It didn't bother me at all that I was not able to actually experience the meal, well, not *too* much.

After he had finished eating, he got a refill on his coffee and we 'talked' about what our next steps would be.

"I think the first two things I should be doing is build my strength back up and get a job. We've got most of the cash left from the hospital which will help us for a while. What about the credit cards? Should we use them to rent a hotel room?"

If I had a head, I would've been shaking it. *I don't think so. The police can track the locations where credit cards are used. I think it would be too risky. I'm sure the hospital has notified the police you escaped from a mental hospital and stole the credit cards and cash.*

They're probably going to consider you dangerous and are actively searching for you right now. We need to get out of town as soon as you finish your breakfast.

I glanced out the window that looked out on the parking lot and saw two patrol cars pull up and stop. They didn't have their lights and sirens on, maybe they were just taking a meal break. We couldn't risk it.

Cops are here now! Leave a twenty on the table and walk back to the men's room. There's an emergency exit next to it.

"Won't it be alarmed?" Joshua whispered as he dropped the twenty on the table and causally began walking to the bathroom.

Not anymore. I just disarmed it. Move it! Wait for me on the other side of the park. I'll find you.

Joshua slipped out the emergency exit, quietly closing the door behind him. I 'watched' as the police officers approached the manager and showed him a picture. The manager turned and pointed to where Joshua had been eating. The officer with the sergeant stripes turned to the other three cops; two of them exited through the front door, one going right and the other left. The third one ran to the emergency exit which I had rearmed. When he pushed the door open, the blare of the alarm could be heard everywhere in the diner and the customers dropped their knives and forks and high-tailed it outside. Most of them left without paying for their meals, jumped into their cars and drove off quickly. The manager wasn't amused.

I transported (teleported? Not sure which is more accurate) to where Joshua was on the other side of the park, partially hiding behind a large tree trunk, checking for any police. He jumped when he heard my voice.

We need to get you a long way from here as quickly as possible.

"Damn, Caleb! Give me some warning you're here."

Sorry dude. It couldn't be helped.

I quickly scanned the area close to the park and noted a city bus was coming a few blocks away. It was either the bus or steal a car. I opted for the bus. Josh got on the bus, paid the fare and headed to the back of the half empty bus. I checked the overhead picture of the bus route. I quickly transported (I prefer that term) to each stop to see what was available and settled on the fifth stop which was close to a truck stop, a few miles away from our present position.

I told Joshua my plan. He asked, "Why a truck stop?"

Because I'm hoping we can catch a ride with a trucker heading out of town, hopefully out of state, I answered.

"Why hitch a ride with a trucker, won't he be inclined to turn me in?"

Not if you tip him two hundred bucks, half when you leave and the other half when you get off.

He thought for a few moments as the bus continued on its way, making its planned stops. Then he smiled and said, "For a dead man you sure have some good ideas."

It's a gift, I replied.

CHAPTER 4

On the Road Again—Caleb

An hour later, we were riding in the cab of a late model Mack Truck Anthem heading west. A couple of hours later, Joshua retired into the sleeper compartment and went sound asleep. Since I didn't sleep, I began to consider our next steps.

I decided on Oxford, Mississippi, hometown for the University of Mississippi. It was two states away from Atlanta, about an eight-hour drive with a couple of stops in Alabama before crossing over into Mississippi. It would take our driver, Howard, at least another three days of traveling to reach his final destination in San Diego.

Two hours out from Oxford, Joshua had woken up from his six-hour nap, refreshed but hungry. He sat quietly in the passenger seat and munched on a couple of Ding Dongs Howard shared with him, washed down with a bottle of water.

It was late afternoon as I began to quietly share my thoughts with him as Howard piloted the big rig into what was left of a sunny day. *I think we should get off in Oxford. It's the next stop on Howard's route. Do you remember visiting there just before we graduated from high school?*

Joshua made a show of putting in his ear buds and pretending to listen to music on his smart phone. He nodded in time to the imaginary music to let me know he remembered our visit. We had both received offers for football scholarships to the University of Mississippi. We had spent a couple of days visiting the campus. It had been the only school to offer both of us scholarships.

Our parents didn't have enough money to pay for one of us to attend a university let alone both of us. But several of our high school friends had chosen to join the military and they were pressuring us to join too. Our father suggested we sign up for the Marines and do one tour, then go to school on the GI Bill once the tour was over. That way we could still go to whatever college we wanted and maybe still play football. That's what we decided to do.

When we arrived in Oxford the sun was just setting. Howard dropped us off near the university and Joshua gave him the second hundred dollars, thanked him for the use of his sleeper and waved good-bye. The next order of business was to get my brother fed. I remembered a college hangout we visited on our scholarship visit five years ago. They had great Steakburgers and it was only few blocks away. After a short walk we were at the Steak and Shake.

Dinner at Steak and Shake—Joshua

It had literally been years since I'd had a Steakburger and the aroma of the food being cooked made my mouth water before I'd sat down in the nearest booth. The place was close to being at capacity and while we waited for the server to take my order, I did a quick check of the customers. About eighty percent were college aged students. I was young enough to be a grad student (but not smart enough) to fit in with the majority. The noise level of the conversations bordered on deafening but I didn't have to worry about anyone wondering why I was talking into my smart phone; at least half the crowd was speaking into their phones.

The remaining twenty percent could have been instructors or professors or maybe coaches for the numerous sports teams Ole Miss had for their athletic programs. I noticed several very large young men sitting at a number of tables that had been pushed together. I counted about a dozen all of whom were wearing lettermen jackets with the university's logo of a landshark. There were also a couple of older men whom I assumed were coaches.

When a very attractive young lady slipped into my booth directly across from me, I forgot about the jocks; she had my complete attention. She was wearing a cheerleader's outfit which also had the landshark logo emblazoned on her chest. "How's it hanging, big guy. What would you like to eat?" she flashed me a friendly smile and waited for me to order.

I didn't hesitate, "I want two large prime Steakburger combos and add bacon, two strawberry shakes and two large Coke Zeros."

"Do you want me to hold the second Steakburger until your friend joins you?" she asked.

I almost said, 'No my brother is a spirit, he doesn't eat.' Fortunately, Caleb sensed what I was about to say. *Don't say it!*

I shook my head at her and answered, "No, it's all for me."

"Wow!" she said, raising her eyebrows in mock surprise. "You're a big eater. I like that in a guy."

I felt embarrassed and fumbled for something to say. "I had to skip lunch," was all I could manage.

She giggled and slid out of the booth. "I'll bring your order in a flash, big guy. I don't want you wasting away from hunger." She squeezed my shoulder as she passed by, heading for the kitchen.

She was true to her word, it seemed like only a few minutes passed and she returned to our booth with a large tray covered with all my food and drinks. "Just let me know if you need a refill on your drinks or need to order more food, big guy." She winked at me with her baby blue eyes and flounced away to take more orders from new customers.

I began eating with gusto; everything tasted fantastic. While I was stuffing my face, Caleb was scanning the crowd.

Josh, stop stuffing your face for a few seconds and casually turn to look at the guys with the lettermen jackets. Do you see the older men? Do any of them look familiar to you?

My mouth was full of juicy burger and I continued to chew without turning my head. Caleb was impatient.

For crying out loud, you can't be that hungry. Look at the oldest guy. Do you recognize him?

I managed a quick glance and said, "No," and kept on chewing.

I think he's the coach who took us on the campus tour when we were thinking about football scholarships. Take another look.

I finished chewing, took a sip of milkshake and slowly turned my head to look at him. Caleb was right, he was the coach and he was staring at me. "What should I do?"

Keep eating. I want to see what he does.

As I finished the first burger and started in on the second one, Caleb gave me a running commentary on what the coach and his players were doing. Before I finished the second sandwich, Caleb 'said,' *They're getting ready to leave...The coach is coming this way. I think he recognized you. Keep cool.*

The coach, I couldn't remember his name, came up beside me and stopped. "Excuse me young man. Aren't you one of the Brown twins we offered a football scholarship to several years ago?"

A cold chill ran down my spine, busted! Caleb said, *Turn your head and smile at him. Stand up and say hello.*

I turned my head and looked up at him, smiled and stood up. "Hello coach, I can't believe you remember me. It's good to see you again." I offered my hand and he shook it.

"My God, you've gotten even bigger. Which one are you, Caleb or Joshua?"

"I'm Joshua. I have to apologize, I don't remember your name, sir."

"Just call me Trevor," he said and smiled broadly. "Are you by yourself? I thought you and your twin were always together."

I froze for a moment. *What should I tell him, Caleb?*

Tell him I died in Kabul, but no details.

"Caleb was killed in Afghanistan over a year ago. It's just me now."

Coach Trevor's smile turned to a look of horror. "Oh my God. I'm so sorry to hear that. That's terrible, really terrible. I'm so sorry for your loss." He reached into his pocket and handed me a card with his phone number on it. "Sit down and finish your dinner but please call me tomorrow morning. I'd like to talk with you some more."

I nodded and sat back down and watched him and a couple of his players as they left the restaurant. *What do we do now, Caleb?*

Do you realized what just happened? he asked.

"Yeah, we're busted. We need to find another truck and..."

No! not that. You just contacted me by telepathy.

I did? I guess I did. Big wow. I thought to him sarcastically.

Yes! gigantic wow. And we may find out meeting the coach is just what the doctor ordered.

CHAPTER 5

Early to Bed, Early to Rise—Caleb

We found an inexpensive motel near campus. Joshua was concerned that the coach was going to turn him in to the local Oxford police and he would be sent back to the Looney Bin in Atlanta. I was pretty sure he wouldn't, in fact I saw this as a potential opportunity for him. We discussed this for about an hour and I think he was coming around. At least I convinced him not to panic.

We watched TV for a while but the big meal at Steak and Shake had made him drowsy. He said, "I'm going to take a shower and turn in for the night. I'll call the coach tomorrow morning. I hope you're right about him."

Okay, now repeat all that with telepathy. You need to practice that approach with me until it becomes second nature. You won't be able to use the smartphone ploy very often.

"But, I'm tired now, Let's start tomorrow," he whined.

Toughen up, Marine! I snarled at him, at least it was my attempt at telepathic snarling. *It will only take you a few seconds.*

Okay, okay! I get it. Now leave me alone, you big meanie, he transmitted back to me with what I detected to be a smile in his message. I'm not sure that makes any sense.

While my brother slept, I considered our options. To my way of thinking, there was the remote possibility that Joshua could be right. However, the only way we would know for sure was to meet with the coach and feel him out. If it looks like a dead end or worse, we need to look at other options.

Maybe I was getting the cart before the horse. We needed to establish Josh's immediate short-term goals. Then determine if the coach could meet all or most of them. I needed to discuss the goals with Joshua when he woke up. I saw them as the following, not in any order of priority:

1. Find a safe place to stay for at least six months
2. Find a job he could do to pay for his room and board
3. Physical therapy to regain his strength and flexibility

He woke early, it was a few minutes before sunrise. His first words were, "I'm starving. Do you think Steak and Shake serves breakfast?"

Telepathy, please.

"Oh crap," he snapped. *I'm starving. Do you think Steak and Shake serves breakfast? Is that better?*

I'm not sure if they serve breakfast, I replied, happy to hear his appetite was back. Then I noticed I shared his hunger. In fact I couldn't wait for him to eat so I would also feel full. *If I remember correctly...*

...there's an IHOP not too far from here, he finished. Just like old times. I would be smiling now if I had a mouth but my feeling of happiness was real.

It didn't take him long and we were out the door, walking to the restaurant. It turned out, it was a little further than we remembered. I was pleased to see that Joshua was able to walk for an hour without showing any signs of fatigue.

It was early and the restaurant had only a few customers. My brother ordered his usual Lumberjack Slam, coffee and orange juice. We began our telepathic conversation regarding our goals while we waited for his meal. When the food arrived, we discovered another benefit to being telepathic; he could eat and communicate with me at the same time. He continued to shovel in his pancakes, eggs, sausage and ham while we 'talked.' His fork never stopped moving and neither did our conversation.

An added benefit for me was that I also got to savor the aroma and taste of the food and my feeling of hunger disappeared, replaced by the feeling of fullness in my belly, even without my belly.

By the end of the meal, we had come to an agreement on his goals and he was ready to call the coach and ask for a face-to-face meeting.

Meeting With the Coaches–Joshua

I called the coach after we spent an hour walking back from the IHOP. He seemed very pleased I'd called. He asked if I could meet with him at his office in the Ole Miss Department of Athletics/Football. He wanted to introduce me to some of his staff and make me an offer he defined as, "an offer you can't refuse." I could feel Caleb's joy through our telepathic connection or maybe it was just my own joyful excitement I was feeling.

We arrived at the university an hour later and were escorted by a grad student who introduced herself as Gloria. Caleb agreed it was a good omen to meet a girl with our mother's name.

Gloria took us to a large multipurpose room next to their weight training facility. We took a quick peek and Gloria said it was the best weight training facility in the SEC. "The coaches claim we have a hundred tons of iron and our athletes lift every ounce of it every day. That's a whole lot of iron pumping,"

I marveled. "How many weight training coaches do you have?"

"Not sure," she answered. "They say they have a ton of coaches but I think they're just joking."

When we walked into the multipurpose room, I was surprised to see about a dozen men and women who stood up as we entered. Coach Trevor, the head football coach, introduced them all from assistant coaches down to a few of the grunts like Gloria. The last one to be introduced was Ken Blakely, the head weight training coach. Ken and his assistants handled weight training for all the various sports. Now that spring football was starting, he was focused on building the strength and agility of the football players. There were close to a hundred potential players on the football roster, from seasoned players all the way to new high school graduates who were fighting for a place on the Ole Miss squad.

Coach Trevor provided some background on me and my brother. "About five years ago, Joshua and his twin brother Caleb were both offered football scholarships to Ole Miss. They were all-state tackles on a 6A high school team that won the state title their senior year. They were both ranked in the top ten of high school offensive tackles nationwide that year. Unsurprisingly, they were tied for fifth place in the rankings.

"Much to our unhappy surprise, they decided to join the Marines instead of accepting our scholarship. They wrote a letter to me I will always remember. They thanked us for inviting them to visit our campus and said they were overwhelmed at our offer and they would have loved to have accepted it. However, they felt an obligation to serve their country and would be enlisting in the United States Marine Corps just as their father had done during the Vietnam War. They closed with the following words, 'We ask you, your staff and your players for your prayers that our Lord guide and protect us during our tour of duty. When it's over, we would both like to revisit your offer, if you're so inclined. Good luck to you, your staff and your players. Ole Miss will remain the only university we would want to play for.' It was signed, 'Respectfully, Joshua and Caleb Brown, PS: Go Landsharks.'"

I looked at Coach Trevor, there were tears running down his cheeks. Many of his staff were just as emotionally touched. The coach asked me a question. "Joshua, would you share with us what happened to your brother, Caleb?"

I was beginning to choke up but managed to say, "He was killed by an IED in Kabul at the end of our second tour."

I could hear the gasps of several of the people in the room followed by the coach asking me, "And how have you been since then?"

At first, I hung my head and shook it slowly, not wanting to tell them of the trauma I had gone through but I heard Caleb's voice in my head. *Tell him, Josh. Tell him what you went through but don't tell him about me.* I raised my head and said with a weak voice, "I've been in a VA hospital, diagnosed with extreme PTSD for the last year, doped up on meds and slowly losing my mind. I escaped from the hospital in Atlanta yesterday. I ended up here last night."

"Why here, Joshua? Why did you stop here in Oxford?" the coach said it with such compassion, I had to answer.

The dam that had been holding my emotions in check broke. I buried my face in my hands and said through my sobbing, "Because I had nowhere else to go!"

The Offer—Coach Trevor

We took a short break to allow Joshua to compose himself and to excuse those from my staff that had other commitments. To their credit, each one of them had a kind word for Joshua as they left. To tell the truth, I was shaken too. What a tragedy Joshua had endured. On the brighter side, I was glad that we might help to relieve him of some of his pain and get him back on track, whether it was football or whatever he chose to do.

We moved from the multipurpose room into my office. I had asked Ken Blakely and Gloria Rodriguez to join Joshua and myself. I had ordered some snacks and drinks and they were placed on the small conference table next to my desk. When everybody was seated and served, I got to it.

"First, I want to thank you Joshua for sharing with us. That took a tremendous amount of inner strength and courage."

The young man just nodded his head in thanks but said nothing.

"We'd like to make you an offer and before you ask, it's not for a full ride scholarship to play football at Ole Miss."

That brought a smile to his face and he replied, "Ah shucks, coach. I was getting all pumped about suiting up and hitting the grid iron."

That brought a chuckle to all of us. What a quick wit for someone who had suffered so much.

"Ken, why don't you fill him in on what we would like to offer him?"

Ken nodded and got to the point quickly. "I just lost one of my strength coaches to an unfortunate accident. He decided to go to work for another university that shall remain nameless, except it is based in Mississippi and considered our rival.

That brought another smile to Joshua's face. Ken continued, "I have to confess, I did an internet search regarding your familiarity with weight training. I had no idea of all the awards you had won while in high school and on active duty in the Marines. You obviously know your way around heavy iron. My question to you is, would you be interested in leading the weight training for our offensive linemen during spring training? Before you decide, I need to let you know you would be expected to follow the training syllabus. Gloria would be keeping stats on all of the players and would report to you and me with the results. Are you interested?"

"Yes!" he answered enthusiastically. "I'm absolutely interested. When can I start?"

"How about tomorrow morning at six. in the weight training facility? Gloria will explain the routine to you," Ken replied.

"Can I get a copy of the syllabus to read before I report?"

Ken just smiled at him, then asked, "Don't you want to know about how much the job pays or where you will live or eat?"

"Okay, I guess I should know about that too but being prepared is the most important thing to me."

Ken turned to Coach Trevor and just shook his head. "I wish all my trainers were this dedicated and enthusiastic." He turned back to Joshua and said, "I want you to move into our football facility. You'll have your own private quarters and you will take your meals with the team, also at the facilities. The syllabus stays in your room. It isn't to leave our training facility. You can move into your quarters tonight if you want. Gloria will make the arrangements and assist you with the move. Any questions?"

Joshua paused and said nothing for a few seconds before answering, "Thank you all for this opportunity, I won't let you down. You have my word."

CHAPTER 6

Movin' On Up—Joshua

Gloria offered to get a couple of the football players to help me move. I had to tell her I had nothing to move, just the clothes on my back and a toiletry kit I'd bought at a local drug store.

At Caleb's suggestion, I'd gotten rid of the three credit cards we'd 'borrowed' from the Atlanta VA Hospital. We mailed them to the hospital from a mail box in Atlanta before hitching the ride with Howard the trucker. We kept the thousand dollars 'donation' from the hospital's doctors. By the time we moved into the Jock Dorm (that's what Gloria called it), we were down to a little over six hundred bucks after I'd bought several meals, paid off Howard and bought my toiletry kit.

Gloria took me to my quarters, gave me keys and an envelope with a thousand dollar advance on my salary. I still had no idea how much I was going to make. To be honest, I really didn't care. I was happy with a place to stay and all the food I could eat. My bonus was to be working in a weight training facility where I could get my strength back.

Caleb accompanied me to the athlete's dining hall. Those on scholarships have the option of eating three meals a day in the dining hall or going off campus to eat at restaurants. Walk on, non-scholarship athletes, weren't permitted to eat in the dining hall. They weren't permitted to live in the Jock Dorm either. Coaches and the staff could eat at the dining hall but seldom did. I learned all this from Gloria who was considered part of Coach Trevor's staff. She also resided in the women's part of the dorm.

To some degree, the athletes tended to be lumped into groups depending on the sport they competed in. The dorm was set up that way and the dining hall seemed to gravitate to the same grouping.

I went through the cafeteria line and piled the food onto a large metal tray until it looked like it would be dripping off the sides. Caleb was in my head. *I realize you've got your appetite back but don't go all piggy on me. You can always go back for seconds, you know.*

I sat down at a table without replying and began eating. *This isn't half bad. Almost as good as the steak burgers I had yesterday.*

You're not the only big eater, he thought to me. *Check out the two guys across from us. They both have two trays overflowing with…it looks like they have some of everything on their trays.*

We watched as they devoured their food and finished both trays before I was done with mine. When they stood up and began walking to the conveyor belt I could see they weren't human, they were alien monsters, one white and one black. Both were at least six ten and I guessed their weight at around four hundred pounds, unfortunately, much of that was fat. They had been sitting at one of the football tables and Caleb and I both assumed they were offensive tackles.

When they returned their trays to a conveyor belt which slowly propelled the trays into a hole in the wall, they turned back and walked to our table. *Stay frosty, I smell trouble coming,* thought Caleb.

The white boy spoke first; he had a very pronounced southern drawl. "Are y'all the new weight trainer we been hearin' 'bout? Ex-Marine and all dat?"

I'll watch the black kid, you take the white porker. Shut him down quick, Caleb thought.

I stood slowly and for the first time in my life, I had to look up to see a white boy's eyes. In the deepest voice I could generate I said, "You got that wrong, big guy. Once you're a Marine you're always a Marine. And yes, I will be your strength trainer. By the looks of you and your friend I'd say both of you need to lose about forty pounds before the season starts. Report to me thirty minutes early tomorrow morning."

"You can't speak to me like…" he started to say more but I stepped quickly towards him until we were nose to nose (actually it was more like my nose to his neck) and shouted in my best drill sergeant voice, "DON'T YOU EVER TALK BACK TO ME. TRY THAT AGAIN AND YOU ARE OUT OF HERE. DO YOU GET ME?"

The entire dining room went silent as the white boy's knees buckled and he stepped back. I stepped closer to him with clenched fists on my hips keeping him off balance as I repeated my question, but this time in a low menacing tone. "Do you get me, mister?"

He collapsed into a chair, nodding his head, unable to speak. When he found his voice, he whined, "Yes sir, I get you."

"Don't ever call me sir again. Sir is for officers. You will address me as sergeant, understood?"

"Yeah…I mean, yes I understand…Sergeant."

"Now, take your friend and get out of my face so I can finish my dinner. And you better not be late for training tomorrow morning."

After the two behemoths had left the dining room there was silence for about ten seconds and I began to finish my food. I noticed the sounds of chairs scraping on the floor as people pushed back from their tables; they began to applaud, then cheered until the dining room rocked.

Gloria came running up to me from a table filled with her girlfriends. She had to yell to be heard above the din. "You're our new hero. Those two monsters are bullies and no one had the balls to stand up to them. You really let them have it. Thank you so much."

New Job, Old Traditions—Joshua

It is important to establish a rep in a new job. Thanks to what happened in the dining hall, I had helped solidify mine: Bad Ass Marine Sergeant and former High School All American Football Player. The difficult part was to maintain that rep and build on it as soon as possible. I had a couple of ideas on how to do that and I was looking forward to trying them out.

Bright and early the next morning, around 0600 hours, I made sure I was the first one in the weight training facility. Caleb had 'volunteered' to check on the two behemoths to make sure they reported early while I went over how I was going to structure my day at the office. The two giants were right on time and by the looks of them they had started working out early; their workout gear was drenched in sweat.

Ken Blakely, now my boss, introduced me to the potential offensive linemen, referred to as the O-line. There were a couple of dozen of them; by the start of the season, half of them would be gone. At least that was what I was told. Player attrition is high in the elite colleges. Some players just quit after they think they don't have a chance of making the squad, others get injured and have to leave and still others transfer to a different college where they think they have a better chance of getting more playing time.

About half of the O-line were seasoned players. A few were already slotted in as starters but once practice begins anything can happen. Six of the men I would be training were right out of high school and on full-ride scholarships. That included my two giant buddies; Caleb had named them Tweddle Dumb and Tweddle Dumber.

Once the introductions were complete, my boss left. It was my turn to speak. I needed to make a few things clear. "According to SEC rules, today is our first official day of strength training. I'm sure some of you have been training at local gyms instead and I appreciate your devotion to iron. Some of you have already been doing weight training for years, many began in middle school, for sure all of you pumped iron in high school and continued in college. Most of you have already established your own training curriculum. All that is going to change, at least some of it will change.

"My title is Strength Trainer but that is only a part of what we will be doing. We will also be doing speed training, agility training and endurance training. Those of you coming in from high school were probably all state selections. Sadly, many of you got by being big and strong. Your idea of a good block on a defensive lineman was to stand in front of him. That isn't going to work in college ball. You need to be strong, fast and sneaky. We will be training you on all factors that will make you better O-linemen.

"The next few days we will be evaluating your present condition. Based on what I see we will design your specific training program. Let's get to it. Everyone outside on the track. It's a beautiful day in Oxford, Mississippi. Your goal is to jog two miles in under fifteen minutes. No one walks. Anyone walking during the two miles will be assigned a remedial training program. Gloria will be recording your individual times and watching for walkers."

I turned to Gloria but noticed some of them were just standing around waiting for…something. I turned to them and put on my drill sergeant voice, "WHY ARE YOU STANDING HERE? ***START RUNNING NOW!***"

All of them sprinted out the door and onto the track. Gloria ran after them with her clip- board and stopwatch. I heard her laugh to one of her friends, "This is going to be so much fun!"

Twenty minutes later, they began returning from the track. Some looked exhausted, a few looked like they had just had a relaxing walk in the park. Ten minutes after that, Gloria came staggering in helping to support the white giant, his black brother was on the other side keeping him from falling. They attempted to lower him to a bench but his legs gave out and he fell to the floor, apparently unconscious.

I ignored him and asked Gloria, "How did the times look?"

She seemed surprised I wasn't looking after Buford (so help me, his name was really Buford T. Justice named for a movie character from the 1977 movie *Smokey and the Bandit,* his daddy's favorite movie, I found out later). Gloria handed me the clipboard and I quickly scanned it.

Everyone but the two behemoths had made the cut off of fifteen minutes. The two best times were around twelve minutes and I congratulated both men. Meanwhile, Buford had barely regained consciousness and was beginning to moan. His partner in crime, the black giant named Charlie Pride (another famous name! What is it with these people? Then I remembered how Caleb and I got our names. I mentally moved on). Anyway, Charlie was sitting on the bench breathing heavy with sweat pouring down his face. He didn't look too good either. Gloria said he stopped jogging to help Buford cross the finish line, otherwise he would have made the time cut. She took his pulse and it was nearly 250!

I took a cold bottle of water and went over to Charlie and offered him the water. He was too exhausted to speak but nodded his head in thanks and took a long swallow then splashed some water onto his face. I told Gloria to get one of our medics to check him out as soon as possible.

I got another bottle of water and walked over to the whining Buford and rolled him over onto his back. His eyes were closed and I poured some of the cold water onto his face. His eyes snapped open and so did his mouth and I poured some water into his mouth. He tried to swallow but began sputtering and choking. I reached down and took his pulse, it was barely over 120. I placed my hand on his forehead and it was relatively cool.

"You look in pretty bad shape, Buford. How do you feel?

"Terrible, Coa…Sergeant. Am I gonna die?"

"Well son, we all gotta die sometime. Maybe it's your time."

Buford's eyes opened wide in terror. "Oh no. It can't be that bad."

I shook my head and said, "I think I might be able to save you, son," as I kneeled down and began licking my lips, leaned in until I was close enough to kiss him. "Only my mouth to your mouth will save you. Open wide."

Buford's mouth slammed shut and he turned his head and screamed, "I be fine now. Don't need no mouth to mouth. I can get up now. I feel much better. Please let me up," he cried as he crawled away from me.

I stood up and looked at him in disgust. "Get your things and get out of my sight."

Without looking at me, he climbed to his feet and stumbled his way to the locker room, never once offering any thanks to his supposed friend Charlie, or Gloria for trying to help him. He was faking it, all of it.

After we were done for the day, I reported to Ken what had happened and stressed that I thought Buford should have his scholarship rescinded and be sent packing.

Without hesitation, my boss agreed. Buford was gone that night. His 'friend' took a day off to recoup and returned to the program.

CHAPTER 7

What, Me Worry?—Caleb

While Joshua was working with the O-line, I was busy covering our trail. I needed to find out if the police were still after us. And if they were, how could we get them off our backs?

Since we returned the credit cards, the only crime I thought we could be charged for was stealing cash but I wasn't sure the doctors ever filed charges with the police, maybe they didn't even realize we'd taken their money. They were rich, at least by our standards. I think the least amount of money I found in their wallets was around a thousand dollars, who's going to miss a hundred or two?

I was more concerned if the Atlanta police would consider an escaped patient from a mental hospital as a threat to the community. Since they never found us, would they have brought in the state police? If they thought he might have left the state, would the FBI get involved? I hardly thought so but I wasn't sure. What about the NCIS? Would someone like Special Agent Gibbs be searching for Joshua? I seriously doubted it but I thought it could make for an interesting episode for the TV series.

The bottom line was that I didn't have access to police records; I had something almost as good: the internet. I hadn't tried it yet but if my ability to manipulate things allowed me to open lockers, I was betting I could access the internet from the computer in Joshua's quarters. Thanks to the university for providing state of the art computers in each of the player's dorm rooms.

While Joshua was busy with his O-linemen, I had his room all to myself. I wasn't sure exactly how to use the computer. They were state of the art systems and could be voice activated, which was of no use to me since I didn't have a voice. I could use the keyboard but

I wasn't sure how to type. Did I have to think each letter? That seemed like it would take forever. A quick attempt confirmed my fears, not to mention I wasn't the most accurate speller which led to even more delays. I didn't want to wait around for Joshua to be my data entry person. I was pretty sure he had better things to do. I wasn't sure what to do which led to frustration.

Suddenly, I was back in my synthetic wonderland with a fake body and preppy clothes. My company commander was waiting for me, dressed in his own preppy outfit. "What do you need Caleb? Why did you contact me?"

"I wasn't aware I called you."

"You're wasting my time. What do you need?" He seemed annoyed by my comment.

"I need to be able to enter data into a desktop computer? I'm not very good at typing."

He shook his head in exasperation, "Is that all? Is it a PC or an Apple?"

I wasn't sure, but I said, "A PC."

"Fine, 'speak' to it the same way you communicate with your brother. Think of how Commander Spock spoke to the Enterprise computer system."

"It's that easy?" I was amazed.

"Don't bother me with this trivial stuff." He left in a huff and wonderland disappeared.

I approached the computer and using my Mr. Spock voice ordered, *Computer, find all references to Joshua Brown from the time he was admitted to the VA Hospital in Atlanta, Georgia, until present date.*

In my mind, I was sure I heard the computer respond, 'Working,' as reams of data began scrolling up on my monitor.

The good news was there were no warrants for Joshua's arrest. In a news report from the hospital, Joshua Brown wasn't considered violent or dangerous. They had no idea how he left the facility and none of the hospital staff was injured. Nothing was mentioned regarding any theft of money or clothes. They requested if anyone spotted him, to contact the hospital. They felt he still needed treatment.

There was nothing from the state police, FBI or NCIS. It sounded like we were home free, at least for the near future. That was good enough for now.

But what about the long term? Lifting weights had always been a hobby for us both. I don't think Joshua ever thought about it being his dream job. Of course, I was ecstatic he was getting paid to get his strength back. I know he was really enjoying working with a team again and football had always been our sport of choice. Wrestling was our second choice and we never would have gotten into it if our high school football coach hadn't also been the assistant wrestling coach.

I will never forget his words at the end of our freshman year, "You twins are big and strong but you have to learn how to go one-on-one against the defensive end in front of you. Wrestling is the best way I know to get that experience. So you both either sign up for wrestling or you don't play football."

Our sophomore year we lost every wrestling match we had but by the time we were seniors we finished first and second at the state meet. Joshua beat me in overtime. I told him I let him win because he had such a fragile ego. Of course, that wasn't true. My backup story was that I slipped on a wet spot on the mat and he was able to escape with three seconds left in the second overtime. That might have been true, probably not.

In college, very few individuals participate in more than one sport. The last one I remember was Curley Culp. He was an All-American football player for Arizona State University who also won the NCAA heavyweight wrestling championship. I think it was way back in the day, maybe 1967. He ended up playing defensive middle guard for several NFL teams. Nobody else has ever come close to Curley.

However, there were a few others, Terry Baker at Oregon State won the Heisman in the early 60s and was the point guard for the Beavers basketball team the same year they played in the NCAA Final Four. Oh yeah, how could I forget Bo Jackson? He was a star running back in the NFL with the Oakland Raiders as well as well as a great outfielder in the MLB in the 80s and 90s. But these were exceptions, even back in the day. Now, if you're a college football player, it's a year round activity.

I knew Joshua would be an excellent coach and he could continue for as long as he wanted. I just wanted to make sure he was back to his old self, both physically and mentally, before we left Ole Miss.

<u>Remembering My Death…Again—Caleb</u>

There are similarities between being a member of a Marine squad and playing on a football team. It's the way you bond together. In football, if you don't have that sense of team, you don't win many games. If a Marine squad doesn't bond, you could lose your life. And many of us did.

I believe that sense of bonding comes from trust. If you trust your team members to execute their individual assignments to the fullest extent possible, with full power and speed, most of the time you win. But not always.

I relived my death in great detail numerous times. My squad's assignment was to clear a specific four-block area. That meant to capture or kill any Taliban terrorists we came across. We had been assigned similar Missions; this was nothing new but not as easy as it sounds.

First of all, the four blocks were part of a war zone. Death and destruction had rained down on those four blocks numerous times but the locals kept returning to salvage what remained of their homes and businesses. Secondly, It was nearly impossible to tell the Taliban from the locals. They dressed alike, spoke the same foreign language and swore to Allah they never hurt anyone. Our Standard Operating Procedure, or SOP if you prefer, was to capture every person you come across, women and children included, search them for weapons and question them thoroughly. If they gave us any indication they were lying, we were to restrain them and send them back to base camp for further interrogation by the 'experts.' If they ran or attacked us, we killed them.

Some of you reading this may be shocked by this level of violence. I know I was. I never got used to it. Fortunately, I never had to take part in killing an escaping prisoner. I did have to beat the daylights out of a few of them. It turned out they were either Taliban or Taliban sympathizers.

The day I died, I did everything by the book but it wasn't enough. One of my squad members shot the local who used his cell phone to detonate the IED that ended my life. He was shot less than a second before he detonated the bomb. When the bullet struck him he was killed instantly, unfortunately he had his thumb on the trigger. His dead body spasmed, resulting in his corpse pushing the button, killing Master Sergeant Caleb Brown.

Power To The People—Joshua

I really enjoyed being a strength coach at Ole Miss. I have to admit most of it was new to me. I also really liked being a gym rat when I wasn't working with the O-linemen. A little over two months had passed since I started my own weight training and I was back to about ninety percent of my pre-war strength. Some days it was a challenge and Caleb was a huge help. We mentally discussed all kinds of things regarding the best way to train college level players; they were so much bigger and stronger than we were when we played high school ball.

And smarter too, Caleb added. *They have to be; the blocking schemes are a lot more complicated now. Run blocking requires quickness and speed along with strength.*

I nodded my head in agreement and added, *Remember what our drill instructors taught us during basic training? They called it explosive power, a combination of strength, speed and agility. Do you remember when they brought in the Israeli Drill Instructor to show us hand-to-hand combat techniques? What did they call it?*

Caleb replied, *It's called Krav Maga. Do you remember the three principles?*

Strike first, strike fast and strike strong. How could I forget? I was his practice dummy; he knocked me on my ass every time I tried to attack him. What was his name? I thought to Caleb.

Major Gad Dagan, a good Jewish boy and an elite class fighter, he responded. *Don't forget he knocked all of us on our butts, not just yours. I was sore for a week but that training sure came in handy during our tours in Afghanistan.*

There was a short pause, then both of us 'said' at the same time, *We need to incorporate Krav Maga into O-linemen training.*

CHAPTER 8

It's Not Your Father's Martial Arts—Joshua

The next day, I spoke to my boss. Ken asked me for a demonstration. After I had knocked him down several times, he suggested we talk to Coach Trevor. Coach Blakely contacted Coach Trevor and set up a time for a demonstration. The head coach declined my offer to be my subject for the demonstration after hearing what happened to Ken. Instead he picked up two of the senior defensive ends. The demonstration consisted of five attempts by each DE separately, then five more by both of them attacking at once. I was a little concerned I might look like an idiot in front of everyone, after all, I still wasn't in peak shape but my adrenaline kicked in. The demo was done in workout gear on a wrestling mat in front of most of the line coaches and a large number of the entire squad. I felt like I was stepping into an MMA match. There was no bell, instead the starting quarterback would bark out signals simulating an actual play in a game, a center would snap the ball to him and the DE would try to get to the quarterback. My job was to keep him from getting to the QB for at least ten seconds.

We took our positions across from each other and crouched into three-point stances. Before the ball was snapped the DE snarled at me and said, "I'm going to hurt you, old man."

"Hut!" The ball was snapped and the DE started his bull rush coming straight at me, his hands coming up to push me into the backfield. I was faster, I took a very quick step forward and drove both hands between his arms as he tried to grab me. I hit him in the chest with everything I had. It lifted him off the ground and he went flying backwards as if shot out of a cannon.

He landed on his back a few feet behind the scrimmage line and didn't get up right away. After a chorus of "WHOA!" rang out, the gym went silent. One of the trainers hurried to make sure the player wasn't injured. He wasn't but boy was he pissed.

The QB said, "Hike on two." The second DE stepped to the line and went into a four-point stance. On the first hut he came roaring across the line and I quickly stepped out of his way. The defensive line coach yelled at him and called him very bad names.

We went again, this time the QB called the snap on the first hut. The DE hesitated just a split second too long. He attempted a swim move and tried to crash by me on my left side, his hesitation permitted me to step under his raised arm and hit him in his exposed ribs, lifting him off the ground, spinning him around and landing him in a heap. To his credit, he bounced up and said, "Let me go again."

Coach Trevor nodded, this time he bull rushed on the first hut, he was angry and angry people make mistakes. He stepped with the wrong foot and I gave him an angled shot to his opposite shoulder. His stepping foot was still up in the air when I hit him, flipping him into a somersault away from the play, he rolled to his feet and continued his attack, throwing an elbow towards my head as he approached the scrimmage line. I had followed him and was right on top of him as he came up. I blocked his elbow and drove my other hand into his armpit lifting him off the ground and onto his back. That took only five seconds and I knew he would try to get up so I waited until he started to get up again and drove into his side with my shoulder knocking his feet out from under him. He stayed down this time.

And so it went. I was five for five for each man separately and four out of five for two-on-one. It was the last one and I was really sucking air at that point. I had put the first man down but I just missed a technique on the second man as he tagged the QB at the count of nine.

Caleb taunted me, *What's the matter, Joshua? You gettin' all old and decrepit, letting these little boys tucker you out.*

Lucky for you, I'm telepathic. Otherwise I wouldn't be able to tell you what I want to say: shut the hell up!

Coach Trevor and a couple of the other coaches approached me as I sat on one of the benches trying to regain my energy. I felt spent. "Joshua, that was the damnedest demonstration I have every had the pleasure to observe. In addition to your strength work with Coach Blakley I would like you to spend some time with both our D-line and O-line coaches. We'd like to find out more about this Krav Maga stuff. Of course there would be an increase in your pay check for this additional activity. Could you come by my office tomorrow after workouts? I'd like to discuss this after you've had a chance to recover from your…demonstration."

That evening after eating in the dining hall, we were getting ready to return to our room when Gloria came running to our table. I had picked an empty table to sit at instead of with the other coaches. I was just too tired to carry on a conversation. She had two very attractive young ladies with her.

Caleb took one look through my eyes and thought, *Uh oh, here come the groupies. You got your pen to sign autographs?*

Before I could respond, the girls were at our table. Gloria introduced them as big fans of mine, which made me pause. How could they be fans? The demonstration was closed to the coaches and players. Gloria informed me one of the players or maybe a coach, had filmed the whole demonstration and put it on YouTube. "It's gone viral," she said. "You're going to be famous."

I heard Caleb groan in the background as the three girls were jumping up and down and giggling. One handed me a screen shot of me knocking down one of the defensive ends. She also handed me a pen and asked me to sign the picture. She said, "Please autograph it, say, 'To Donna, my biggest fan, Love, Coach Joshua.'"

I could hear Caleb making gagging sounds and saying, *Lord have mercy.*

Preparing for the Coaches Meeting—Caleb

The last thing we needed was publicity. We still didn't know for sure if we weren't wanted by any of the various legal agencies. However, having Joshua's YouTube video out there for everyone to see could possibly be a good thing. There's not much we can do about it now. We needed to see what the coach's thoughts were. Joshua had a good point.

I'm really not qualified to teach Krav Maga. Let me check the internet to see if there are any places that teach it in the Oxford area.

He sat in front of the computer for a few seconds lost in thought. I knew exactly what he was thinking. We simultaneously thought projected, *I wonder if Major Gad Dagan would be available. It's a long shot but why not check with him first.*

Before he could begin typing in the search criteria, I began entering the key words: Krav Maga, Major Gad Dagan, Israel Defense Forces.

His hands were poised over the keyboard when the words began showing up in the search window. "Whoa, there's a ghost in my machine," he said.

He let his hands fall into his lap and watched as the search began. A few minutes later, the search was complete. A Lieutenant Colonel Gad Dagan resigned his commission from the Israel Defense Forces a few years ago and opened a number of Krav Maga schools, initially only in Israel. Recently he has franchised schools throughout various European countries, Canada and the United States. He is currently touring in Canada and America holding seminars on the Krav Maga martial art.

We looked for the calendar of the locations where he would be stopping. He was about halfway through his schedule. His last two stops in America were Atlanta and Dallas before heading to Canada.

Simultaneously, we thought, *Atlanta!* Neither of us had any idea why we wanted to go back to Atlanta. At least not at that moment but then another thought occurred to us. *Closure.*

Joshua, at my insistence, approached Coach Trevor without an invitation. "Coach, What you saw in my demonstration was what I remembered from the training I had almost five years ago. The man who trained us in Krav Maga resigned his commission a couple of years ago and now has a number of schools in Europe, Canada and the US. He's going to be in Atlanta for a seminar next week and I'd like to attend. Not only would I benefit from some refresher training and would pass it on to our players, I might be able to convince him to come to Ole Miss and teach our players directly. What do you think?"

The coach's smile got bigger and bigger as Joshua made the pitch. When he was finished, Trevor slammed his hand down on this desk and said, "What a great idea! Why don't you give him a call and reintroduce yourself, sign up for the seminar and see if you can get him to come visit us."

Joshua made the call later that day. We were somewhat surprised at the reaction of the first person he spoke with. "Are you the Ole Miss coach on the YouTube video?"

Cautiously, he replied, "It might be, my name is Joshua Brown and I want to sign up for the seminar in Atlanta next week."

There was a brief pause and a few muffled background sounds, then another voice came on the phone. "Am I speaking to Joshua Brown?" The voice was strong and full of authority with a hint of an accent.

Out of habit when speaking to an officer, Joshua sat up straighter and replied, "Yes sir, this is Joshua Brown."

The voice on the other end of the line said, "The Marine boot, Joshua Brown whom I taught Krav Maga when he was in basic training?"

Joshua looked stunned. "You remember me?"

"Of course not. I taught hundreds of Marines and that was several years ago. I know you from your YouTube demonstration. I want to thank you for that. Because of that video, I've sold out all my remaining seminars. What can I do for you, son?"

"I'd like to attend your seminar in Atlanta next week, if you have any openings left."

"Outstanding," he replied enthusiastically. "For you, no charge and get here a day early. We have a lot to discuss."

"Thank you, Colonel, I'm looking forward to seeing you again."

"Don't call me Colonel. I'm no longer in the IDF."

"Should I call you rabbi, that means teacher doesn't it?"

"God forbid!" he said jokingly. "My students do call me teacher, or sometimes Mr. Dagan- but for you, call me Gad."

The following week we were on our way back to Atlanta.

CHAPTER 9

Leaving on the Midnight Train to Georgia—Caleb

It turned out the best way to get to Atlanta from Oxford was by train. Joshua was so pumped up, we left as soon as he had completed his strength training drills with the O-line for the week. Another strength coach was going to cover for him while he was in Atlanta.

It was getting close to the end of spring training and the team was now focusing on running plays, getting their timing down and for the O-linemen, making sure they knew their blocking assignments for each play in the entire play book, close to a hundred plays. Spring practice would end with a scrimmage between the offense and the defense.

The train to Atlanta didn't leave at midnight but close to it. Joshua was sound asleep before the train left the station. It was an express train which meant it only stopped at the major cities. I was surprised to find out Oxford was considered a major city but I guess in the South things are different. The good news was, even with the stops, we arrived in Atlanta about six hours later. The sun hadn't quite risen but the sky was getting lighter in the east, in spite of the spring showers.

We took a cab from the train station to the Downtown Marriott. Of course we couldn't check in until around noon and Joshua was hungry, so guess where we had breakfast? You're right, at the IHOP a couple of blocks from the hotel.

While Joshua chowed down on the Lumberjack Slam (the only meal he orders at IHOP no matter what time of day) we chatted about what we wanted to accomplish in addition to attending the seminar and asking Rabbi Dagan (I just liked the sound of that title) to come visit Ole Miss.

I wanted to check the local data bases to see if there were any criminal charges due to the YouTube video. Now that Joshua was a celebrity, the local law as well as the hospital might be taking a second look. In addition, I wanted to check if being a celebrity might result in other job opportunities. I had no idea what they might be but, in my heart, I knew Joshua was still basically a Marine. And to tell the truth, so was I.

After a leisurely breakfast we headed back to the Marriott and checked out the possibility of an early check in. The reservation desk clerk said they didn't have any at the present time but he'd put us on his list and text Joshua as soon as a room became available.

Joshua asked where the Krav Maga seminar was going to be held and the clerk directed us to the large ballroom.

As we stepped through the large double doors we were immersed in what appeared to be chaos. A team of men and women were erecting an octagon in the middle of what used to be a dance floor. Other teams were putting together bleachers around the perimeter of the room. Still others were laying down mats between the octagon and the bleachers. On all the walls, huge jumbotrons were being lifted into place by workers using mini-cranes while techies were setting up table after table of computers and supporting equipment with miles of cable being bundled together resembling thick pythons strung out along the floor.

Look for the rabbi. He's bound to be somewhere in this mass of humanity.

Joshua began scanning the room. Half way through his scan he thought to me, *He's over on the platform under the largest jumbotron. And quit calling him rabbi. I don't think he likes it.*

Relax, bro. You know he can't hear me, don't you?

Joshua ignored me and began walking toward the Krav Maga teacher. When he reached the platform, he called out, "Mr. Dagan?"

The man stop talking to one of the helpers and turned to see who was calling him. When he saw Joshua, a huge smile spread across his face. He jumped down from the platform and extended his hand to Joshua and said, "Sergeant Brown I presume. When I spoke briefly with Coach Trevor yesterday he told me you'd be the largest man in the building and he was right. It's a pleasure to meet you."

While they made small talk, I checked the rabbi out. He was average height, around five feet ten, lean but well-muscled and carried himself like the man in charge. He was dressed in casual clothes, a short-sleeved cotton shirt with the words, Krav Maga Instructor printed on the chest, khaki pants and black high-top Niki shoes. His hair was high and tight, salt and pepper, with more salt than pepper. I noticed when he shook my brother's hand it was firm but not a bone crusher grip. When he spoke, there was no doubt he was in charge.

"Now that I see you in person, I do remember you. It was during your boot camp at Camp Lejeune. You and your brother were the biggest grunts I'd ever had the pleasure of training."

He turned and briefly shouted instructions to the crew on the platform then turned back to Joshua. "Please come with me. I've got half an hour to brief you on what I want to do during the seminar and also discuss the offer from your football coach."

Without comment from Joshua, he turned and headed for a small office located near the entrance. Joshua quickly fell in behind him and had to hurry to keep up. *This guy is a human dynamo,* he thought to me. *All business. I hope we can keep up with him.*

They sat at a small table in the office. Joshua spoke first, "Mr. Dagan, I'm no longer in the Marines. I received a medical discharge from the Corps about a year ago. You don't have to call me sergeant."

"Nonsense," he replied immediately with authority. "Isn't the Corps' motto, 'Once a Marine, Always a Marine?' I plan to introduce you as Sergeant Brown."

"Introduce me? Who are you going to introduce me to?" asked Joshua.

Just listen to the man, Josh. I think he has big plans for you at the seminar, I thought back to him.

An hour later, after we left the rabbi, we headed back to the reservation counter to see where we stood on the early check in list. To our surprise our room was ready. I think the rabbi may have had something to do with us getting into our room so quickly. Joshua's head was spinning. *I'm having a hard time accepting all this. I thought it would be a pleasant conversation but it turns out he's like a used car salesman. I'm not comfortable with the things he wants me to do but on the other hand, if I do them he will do a free training session with the Ole Miss football team. I feel obligated to the team after all they've done for me.*

You're right, the rabbi is a quid pro quo kinda guy. But it's only a one-time event and there could be some interesting benefits for you.

Such as? he asked.

The possibilities are endless. Let's just wait and see, I answered.

That means you don't have any idea, doesn't it?

No, that means there are so many opportunities just waiting for you, I can't remember them all.

You are so full of shi…

There were three loud knocks on the door, interrupting Joshua's crude train of thought.

That could be one of them now. That could be opportunity knocking. I added as he walked to the door.

When he opened it, a Marine in his dress uniform, white gloves and spit shined shoes, stood at ridged attention. Joshua just stood staring at him in shock and confusion until the Marine asked, "Is this the quarters for Master Sergeant Joshua Brown?"

Tell him yes and invite him in, I suggested.

Instead, Joshua answered, "My name is Joshua Brown but I was discharged over a year ago." He began to close the door but the Marine placed his hand on the door and continued. "You have been reassigned to temporary active duty. Here are your orders."

As if he were sleepwalking, my brother extended his hand and took the orders, scanning them as the Marine began speaking again.

"Later this afternoon you will receive a package containing your dress uniform. You are ordered to wear the uniform to the Krav Maga seminars this evening, tomorrow and Sunday. You are ordered to conduct yourself in a manner becoming to the Corps. Semper Fi, Marine." He saluted, did a right face and headed back toward the bank of elevators. The door closed slowly on its own as a dumbfounded Joshua stood staring blankly at the door.

He finally spoke, *How can this be happening? Is this a dream or a nightmare?*

Apparently, the retired lieutenant colonel in the IDF still had friends in the United States Marine Corps. Both Joshua and I believed Josh had been given an honorable discharge from the Corps for medical reasons. Apparently, that hadn't happened. Instead, during an internet search, I discovered it wasn't uncommon for troops suffering from severe PTSD were classified as being on medical leave. If they recovered, they were placed back on active duty, if they didn't recover after an unspecified amount of time, they were given a medical discharge. Since Joshua Brown was considered now to be fully recovered, his orders placing him on temporary active duty were valid and binding. I'm sure the rabbi had something to do with that decision. But who are we to complain, as long as it's only temporary active duty.

Later that afternoon there came another knock on our door. Joshua didn't move, he just thought to me, *Get the door, please.*

Very funny. You don't have to show me you're still Looney Tunes. It's too late for that.

There was a second knock, Joshua stood up and grudgingly walked to the door and opened it. One of the hotel staff wheeled in a garment cart with a clean and pressed Marine dress uniform hanging there; complete with a hat, white gloves and shiny black shoes. All in his size. I wondered where they got his measurements.

There was a note attached to the uniform. It read 'Master Sergeant Joshua Brown, you are hereby ordered to shower and shave, dress in the uniform provided to you and show up front and center at the stage in the hotel's large ballroom promptly at 1500 hours. Do not be late.' It was signed by a Marine general we had never heard of but I was sure it was legitimate.

Without comment, Joshua turned and walked into the bathroom. A few minutes later, I heard the shower running. Promptly at 1500 hours we arrived front and center at the stage in the hotel's large ballroom as ordered by the anonymous Marine general.

CHAPTER 10

Let the Show Begin!—Gad Dagan

I couldn't wait to begin the seminar. Master Sergeant Brown looked terrific in his new uniform. He was all business as I instructed him for the last time on what his role was to be. There were going to be four seminar sessions, one Friday night, two on Saturday and one on Sunday morning. Sunday afternoon the construction team would tear down the whole setup and ship it to Dallas, Texas, for the next scheduled seminar. During the week preceding the Dallas show, some of my instructors and I would spend two days working with the Ole Miss football team.

Having Joshua show up was a gift from God. I was going to make a small fortune from the royalties I'd be getting from ESPN. They had contacted me to televise live tonight's seminar on ESPN2. In addition, they will record and replay it at an undetermined date. My agent is also discussing the possibility of a mini-series of the training we will be doing at Ole Miss. Not only would I make a ton of money from the ESPN contract, we would also profit from the number of new students who would sign up for training because of the publicity. I wondered if I could convince Joshua to travel with my troops and perform at Dallas and the six seminars in Canada.

Promptly one hour later, at 1600 hours, or 4:00 p.m. if you prefer, the seminar began. The bleachers were full and everyone was waiting. I stepped though the curtain and walked to the front of the stage. There was a smattering of applause and a few fans yelling things I couldn't understand but they quieted down as I waited for silence. When I had it, I began.

"Ladies and gentlemen, my name is Gad Dagan and I am a Krav Maga instructor. Welcome to our first seminar in Atlanta. I want to begin by telling those of you who aren't familiar with Krav Maga exactly what it is and what it's not."

I began moving across the stage. I find it more compelling for people to listen if I am moving around. I seldom stand in one place. "Let's begin with what it isn't. It's not a sport. We don't have contests and give out trophies to the winners of 'sparring matches' or performing katas as if we are fighting imaginary opponents. We also don't train children. At my schools, all my schools, we train only people over eighteen years of age."

When I reached the end of the stage, I turned and headed back the other way, continuing making eye contact with as many people as possible. "Now, let me tell you what Krav Maga is."

I stopped walking and paused for effect. "I should add something here. Not all Krav Maga schools are the same. Some do teach children and have sporting contests. I don't for very good reasons.

"What I teach is self-defense. When someone tries to hurt you or capture you or possibly even tries to kill you, being able to defend yourself is my primary concern. Do I guarantee my Krav Maga will always keep you safe? Of course not, but Krav Maga gives you the best chance of surviving.

"Krav Maga isn't for everyone. It can be very violent. When practicing you may get injured. Before I begin teaching any contact activities, I make sure my students are in good enough physical condition. Many have to train for months before they begin contact drills. And to be honest, there have been a number of students I had to turn away because they were more of a danger to themselves than any attacker would be.

"A little background. I began Krav Maga training when I joined the Israel Defense Force, or IDF for short. Everyone in Israel, men and women, has to serve in the IDF when they turn eighteen. All of us are trained to be soldiers, to fight and kill when necessary to defend our country from attack.

"At the time I joined the army, Krav Maga was only taught to soldiers in our military and to Israeli police. It was thought too dangerous to teach to civilians. But now it has become very popular with civilians. Why is that? Because the world has become a dangerous place, not just in battlefields or war zones but across neighborhoods everywhere. The desire to protect ourselves and our families has become a priority for many who have to deal with the threat of violence on a daily basis.

"I'm almost done with the introduction but first I want to let you know we have a special guest with us today. He is going to introduce you to a practical application of Krav Maga. I mentioned we don't usually teach athletes our techniques but this is an exception. I taught our guest and many other Marines the basics of Krav Maga for hand-to-hand combat techniques five years ago. After serving two tours in Afghanistan, he is currently an offensive line coach at Ole Miss and has applied our principals to his linemen to be used to protect not only themselves but also the team's quarterback and running backs. Many of you have seen the YouTube video of not only one-on-one attacks but also multiple attackers. We're going to show you that video in a moment but first let me introduce you to Master Sergeant Joshua Brown, offensive line and strength coach for the Ole Miss Landsharks."

When Joshua stepped out from behind the curtain, the crowd when crazy. They were on their feet applauding and cheering as he walked up to me and shook my hand. He turned and waved at the crowd and waited for them to quiet down. I looked up at him, way up at him, and said, "My God, you are a monster! How big are you?"

"I'm almost six feet seven and I weigh three hundred pounds, give or take a few pounds," he replied.

"Do you remember the Krav Maga training I introduced to you when you were going through basic training?"

He nodded. "How could I have forgotten. You gave me the worst beating I'd ever had. I couldn't believe how a little guy like you could whoop up on a big guy like me but you did. I was never so happy to see an instructor leave camp as when you said good-bye. I was sore for a month after you left."

There was a lot of laughing by the crowd and I paused until it died down, then said, "I see by the YouTube video we are going to show shortly that you retained a considerable amount of your training and applied it well. Why don't you tell everyone what the drill was about?"

As I had coached Joshua, he briefly explained how this was a demonstration intended for the players and coaches to see how Krav Maga techniques could be used to more effectively block opponents. Our technical people had added some musical background, I think it was from an old *Rocky* movie, something about a tiger's eye but I thought it really added to the drama of how effective Krav Maga could be in protecting one's self from attackers.

The video lasted about fifteen minutes. The audience was on its feet screaming and yelling like it was an MMA fight, especially when Joshua was defending himself from two attackers at the same time. Most importantly, it showed in no uncertain terms how effective KM could be for self-defense. When the video ended, I thanked Joshua for his service and for sharing his video with us. He received a standing ovation as he walked off stage.

Once the audience had settled down, I gave a quick overview of what the rest of the seminar would entail, all the time thinking that I had discovered a gold mine when Joshua called and asked if he could attend the seminar. I was a rich man before his call but I was about to become much richer.

Taking the Train Back Home—Joshua

The seminars had been great. Once I was done with my part, I went back to our room and changed from my uniform to workout gear and took part in the training. I joined up with a different instructor for each of the four seminars and each of them made it clear I had a lot to learn. When Caleb and I boarded the train back to Oxford, I was exhausted and really sore. However, I had no regrets or any injuries to speak of.

I had dreaded the thought of getting all dolled up in my dress uniform and pretending to be a Marine but by Sunday it felt very natural. Just like it felt natural to get beat up by students who were half my size. Training with them was a humbling experience but I learned a lot. It was always a lot of fun to watch the audience when a smaller woman would throw me to the mat.

The rabbi (Caleb has me conditioned to using that title for Mr. Dagan. He claims it's his code name.) offered to pay me for my time in Atlanta but I declined. I didn't want him to think I was working for him. When we checked out, I found he had paid for all our expenses. I have no idea if he paid for my dress uniform or the Marines picked up the tab. Caleb and I had discussed if this was a one-time thing or if the government could pull my chain any time they wanted me back on active duty. That was a scary thought but we'd just have to wait and see.

I slept most of the way back to Oxford and felt a little better when Caleb woke me as we rolled into the station. I was still half asleep but I thought I heard music playing as I stumbled down the aisle to the exit.

It was early Sunday evening and it was chilly and raining as I stepped down onto the platform. The music I thought I'd heard started up full-force again. I was shocked fully awake to see the entire Ole Miss marching band. They were playing the school fight song with cheer leaders dancing in front. Behind them was the football team and some of the coaches. Behind them the station was full of alumnae and locals holding banners. I was pretty sure I was still on the train in the middle of a dream. Actually, it was more like a nightmare.

Caleb thought to me, *Welcome home, hero. You're a full-fledged celebrity now. Get your pen out, you have autographs to sign.*

I shook so many hands and signed way too many autographs; my right hand was beginning to cramp. It took the better part of two hours to get back to our room in the jock dorm. Now I was really exhausted but also hungry.

Caleb suggested, *Why don't we hit the Steak and Shake and avoid all the college teeny boppers?* I guessed he felt my hunger and he shared the hungry feeling. Steak and Shake sounded great.

As we headed out the door, I thought to him, *Teeny boppers? Really? That was old when we were young.*

You forget, I live in the past. Everything old is new again.

I smiled. *You're right, Master Yoda. Thank you for sharing your words of wisdom. For I sense the Force is strong within you.*

Caleb declined further banter as I walked briskly in the rain, getting hungrier with every step.

Onward and Upward—Caleb

The rabbi was true to his word. Bright and early Monday morning, he showed up at the Ole Miss training facility. With him were four instructors including the woman who pretty much wiped the mat with Joshua during the seminar. They spent almost two days working with the coaches and players. Of course, Joshua was ready to get beat up again.

I think the two defensive ends who had been Josh's opponents in the YouTube video really enjoyed seeing Joshua getting thrown around, especially by the woman instructor who couldn't have weighed more than 125 pounds. Every time Joshua would get thrown to the ground or fail to make a block on a punch she made, they would snicker and laugh. They stopped laughing when the woman had both of them try to capture her. No bones were broken but both were limping and grimacing for several days after the instructors had left for Dallas to their next seminar.

That training was a huge success. Both the offensive and defensive lines profited greatly by the Krav Maga training as demonstrated when the football season got underway the following fall. Coach Trevor was overjoyed by the team's performance during the season and attributed their success in part to the special training they received from Gad Dagan and his team of instructors.

Spring training ended a month later. We had a decision to make. What were we going to do next? We had several offers. Two came from Coach Trevor. The first was for Joshua to stay on as a full-time coach during the season. The second one was the offer of a football scholarship to play for the team he had been coaching. We found the last offer a huge surprise and Joshua considered it for about a day but then he got an offer from an NFL team. It appeared the Atlanta Falcons needed to replace their nose tackle who had decided to retire due to lingering injuries. They offered Josh an insanely huge signing bonus and a guaranteed salary.

"This is ridiculous!" he yelled out loud. "I haven't played ball in five years and when I did, it was as an offensive tackle not as a defensive lineman. What in the hell are these guys smoking?"

I think the offer that most attracted Joshua was from Gad Dagan. He wanted him to head up the seminar training programs. It would involve him traveling all over the world to introduce Krav Maga self-defense to countries they hadn't already served. The proposed salary was very good, not as good as the Atlanta Falcon's offer but still sizeable. Also, we both liked to travel and this would certainly give us the opportunity to see places we had never been to before.

We pondered these and other lesser offers but in the end none of these options were chosen. Our government had other ideas about how Joshua could best use his talents to the benefit of the USA. Of course, I'm not allowed to discuss the so-called offer or what his responsibilities would be. You might want to think of a black James Bond on steroids.

CHAPTER 11

Uncle Sam Needs You—Caleb

A week had gone by and I could tell Joshua was ready to contact Gad Dagan and accept his offer. There was never any deadline for responding but Joshua was getting antsy to get back to work again. He knew if he accepted Dagan's offer he would have to go through some bone-crushing training but he was up for it. Attending the seminar in Atlanta and the sessions with the Ole Miss football team was a taste of what he was in for.

I was really proud of my brother. He had come so far during the last two years, in a different way, so had I. Never in my wildest fantasies did I ever think I would leave my body and exist as a spirit. Well, actually I didn't leave my body; it was taken from me in the most violent way I can imagine.

At night, when Joshua was sleeping along with the vast majority of the living people around us, I had time to think. What I'm going to reveal to you are secrets but I want to share them with you so you can better understand my existence. When my human body was ripped from me, I initially existed in a state of chaos. I was scared to death, I had no senses. I couldn't see, hear, smell, taste or feel anything but somehow, I was aware of an infinite number of beings like me, spirits detached from their bodies. I wish I could be more specific but not being able to understand my existence terrified me. Everything seemed to be swirling about me. I had no idea how long this went on. Eventually, I became aware the number of detached spirits were decreasing, the sense of chaos was becoming less chaotic. I was encouraged by this for some reason and I focused on this reduction. After what seemed like an eternity there was only me. I was alone in the void. Another eternity passed and I could 'see' a pinpoint of light in the blackness of the void. Slowly, ever so slowly, the pinpoint grew into a window. Through that window I could 'see' a body, lying in a hospital bed. It looked just like me, was it me? I wanted it to be me. I wanted to be human again. I wanted it desperately to be me.

The next instant, it was me. But that me was sound asleep. I was confused. With a start, Joshua woke up and tried to push me out of his body. I fought against him with all my might. One moment it was my body, the next it was his. We struggled back and forth until I realized I was draining his life force. I was killing him. I was killing my own brother! I had to stop. I accepted the fact that I was never going to be human again. Then I heard the voice.

Caleb, you chose wisely. If you had persisted you would have killed your brother. What you didn't realize was if you did kill him you would have ceased to exist as well. You will continue to exist but only in spirit form. You have a challenge ahead of you. You must bond with your brother. In order for that to happen, he has to accept you for what you are. Do you understand?

Who are you? I thought. *Why didn't you reveal this to me sooner? Why did you let me almost kill my brother before you stepped in?*

Think of me as your Spirit Guide. Before I could reveal myself to you, you had to realize what you are and recognize your limitations. Only a few people have done what you have done. You love your brother as much as you love your own existence. You have a long journey ahead of you to complete bonding with him. Persevere, Caleb. It will bring you more joy than you can imagine.

Let me share the first secret: time is for living flesh. Spirits aren't flesh and time works differently for us. I've been led to believe, when Joshua goes to sleep and I don't have anything to think about, the next moment, the sun is rising and he's getting up.

The second secret: spirits don't get any older. When a body dies, its spirit doesn't age beyond that point. The third: when I transport from one place to another, it's instantaneous. Now here is the real freaky part. I can transport to a certain place away from Joshua and stay for a day or a week, maybe a year. When I return to him, it's like only a second has elapsed.

As far as I know, I can't go back in time, at least not yet. Neither can I go into the future, although I've heard from my training spirit I can project how reality will occur for a few moments from the present. As of yet, I haven't been granted that ability and maybe I never will. It all depends on need and justification. Not my need, more like the needs of the spirits. It's very complicated and I'm only beginning to scratch the surface.

Consider all of the above a tutorial on spirit existence. It is incomplete and more will be added later or not, depending on my development.

I'm done for the night. Shutting down now…Oh look! It's morning and someone's knocking on our front door.

It was 0600 hours and Joshua was still fast asleep. I 'yelled' at him, *Joshua, get up. There's someone pounding on our door.*

He rolled out of bed, dressed only in his boxer briefs and stumbled to the door, unbolted the locks and opened the door. Standing in front of him was the same Marine who had delivered his orders. He was still attired in his dress uniform. Now he carried a rather large box. "Master Sergeant Joshua Brown, sorry to disturb you this early but I was ordered to bring you this computer. It will have an encrypted message for you that you are to read and respond to no later than 1000 hours today." He shoved the box into Joshua's hands, did a left face and left.

Joshua closed the door, bolted it, turned, took two steps, placed the box on the coffee table and fell back into his bed. He was instantly asleep. I gave him an hour, then woke him up again.

He was up at 0700 hours, showered, shaved, brushed his teeth and everything else that needs to be done in the bathroom all by 0730 hours. For breakfast, he grabbed a couple of stale, leftover donuts he'd bought yesterday and poured a cup of coffee from the coffee maker in our room which he finished by 0800. Wiping his sticky fingers and donut crumbs from his mouth, he plugged in his new computer. I looked over his shoulder at the message.

It read:

> **To:** Marine Master Sergeant Joshua Brown
> **From:** US Veterans Administration
> **Special Assignments Division**
> **Re:** Required Evaluation
>
> You are required to appear at the address below at the VA Office of Special Assignments in Washington D.C. at the time and date listed below. You will undergo a battery of tests to determine your next assignment. If you fail to appear at the date and time specified below you will be considered AWOL and may be sentenced up to two years in the federal prison at Leavenworth, Kansas.
>
> Transportation will be provided for your trip to WDC as well as accommodations at a hotel close to the VA Office of Special Assignments.
>
> If you have any questions, please reply to this message prior to 1000 hours today.

It was signed by the same Marine general who had returned him to active duty.

I was as surprised as Joshua and a little pissed off at the message. *So, what do you think? This is an ultimatum. I really don't like ultimatums. We escaped from the VA once before, we can do it again if you want.*

A slow smile spread its way across Joshua's face. *I'm curious to find out where this is going. Let's go to DC and I'll take part in their evaluation and see what they have to offer. If we don't like it we can always disappear if we need to.*

I thought for a moment before replying to my brother. I understood where he was coming from but he hadn't really thought it through. *You're right, bro. However, escaping from Uncle Sam maybe a little tougher this time around. They still don't have a clue how you escaped from the hospital in Atlanta. If they truly want you, the security will be a lot tighter than it was at the hospital.*

His smile got broader. *I realize that but they don't know I've got a secret weapon. You and I both know when we set our minds to something, we're going to make it happen and no one, including our Uncle Sam is going to be able to stop us. We are the epitome of the Dynamic Duo.*

That made me chuckle or a reasonable facsimile of a chuckle, *Where you been learning them ten-dollar words, bro? Do you even know what epitome means?*

He laughed and thought to me, *Of course I do. I saw the word in a New Yorker magazine and then looked it up on the internet.*

It was my turn to laugh. *My Oh My! You be readin' the New Yorker? What happened to my down-home brother. Lord save us both from the New Yorker. You read that magazine and soon you be buyin' thousand-dollar shoes.*

Joshua sent an encrypted reply to the orders indicating he had no questions and would be reporting as required to the VA Office of Special Assignments at the date and time required.

Not to burn any bridges, he also contacted Coach Trevor and Gad Dagan and told them he was ordered to Washington DC for an evaluation but he was still considering their offers.

After lunch at Steak and Shake and saying our good-byes to the coaches and players of the Ole Miss football team (that included Gloria who gave Joshua a huge hug and a special kiss on the cheek), we caught a limo ride from Oxford for the 47 mile ride to Tupelo Regional Airport. We took the last flight of the day from Tupelo to the Washington National Airport. A special limo was waiting for us at the airport and took us into the city and dropped us at a very upscale hotel.

We checked into the hotel, had dinner at the hotel dining room and retired to our room. The room was on the twentieth floor and had a great view of the Potomac River. Across the river you could see a portion of Arlington National Cemetery. If I had a body, I would have been feeling chills going down my spine.

I was looking through by brother's eyes and I could feel him beginning to tremble and then the tears came. His tears were for both of us. I vowed to visit my grave site soon, very soon.

CHAPTER 12

Who Are You? We Really Want to Know—Joshua

There were attachments to the encrypted email. There are always attachments to government emails. These attachments were very specific. Joshua wasn't to wear his Marine dress uniform at any time when he was in DC.

For the first part of the evaluation he was instructed to wear business casual. That pretty much left the door open to our imagination. For a Wall Street broker, business casual could mean he can take off his suit coat and loosen his tie. For a city bus driver, it could mean Bermuda shorts and a Diamondback's tank top. We chose somewhere in between; Docker pants, Polo short-sleeve pullover shirt, matching socks and deck shoes.

Once the information gathering part of the evaluation was completed, a physical evaluation would commence. Joshua was ordered to bring workout gear. We weren't sure if that included weight training gear like a lifting belt, knee and elbow wraps, chalk and lifting gloves or perhaps a martial arts gi or even a skin-tight leotard which showed off every crack and crevice in his body.

What about weapons? Was he to bring his own weapons? Would they expect only side arms or want us to include sniper rifles? How about nunchakus and throwing stars or perhaps staffs and escrima sticks? Or should a variety of knives and swords be included? This was getting ridiculous!

One thing we found out about our beloved government was when they sent you instructions they were always vague. Whoever made out Joshua's instructions probably didn't know escrima sticks from chop sticks but if you didn't show up with the proper stuff they would count it against you.

We decided on basic training stuff: sweatpants, shorts, sweatshirt, tank top, sweat socks, a jock, a Ka-Bar knife, Glock 19 and 44 Auto Mag, plus all the ammo needed to stop a platoon of bad guys. If that wasn't enough, he'd have to improvise.

The length of the evaluation wasn't specified but we expected to run at least a few days, maybe a week. It was up to Uncle Sam to decide. It would probably depend on how many other people were being evaluated.

Eval Day 1—Answer All the Questions—Caleb

We arrived exactly on time, 0900 hours at the designated place. It was interesting how we got there. At 0800 hours a call was made to our room that ordered Joshua to be at the curbside to the hotel in ten minutes with his gear. At 0809 we stood outside and waited until a very unusual looking vehicle pulled up into the loading zone. The back door automatically opened and a voice said, "Are you Marine Master Sergeant Joshua Brown?"

"Yes, I'm Joshua Brown," he replied.

"Good morning, Master Sergeant Brown. Please enter the vehicle and place your bag on the seat next to you. The door will close automatically."

We entered the limo and as soon as Joshua sat down, a seat belt automatically encircled him and locked him comfortably into place while the door closed. "Please sit back and relax. The ride to the VA Evaluation Center will take 38 minutes. During that time you may watch a variety of programs on the screen in front of you. Refreshments are located in a console to your left."

The interior was plush but all the windows were blacked out. Joshua asked, "Can I see through the windows please, I want to see outside as you drive?"

"I'm sorry, Master Sergeant, the location of the center is classified."

Joshua began to scowl at the reply. Before he could say anything, I thought to him, *Chill, Josh. I know exactly where we're going. They're going to drive around to make sure they're not being tailed, then drop you off at the Pentagon. Why don't you have one of those donuts and a cup of coffee. They have your favorite, chocolate cake with chocolate frosting.*

How do you know all this? he asked suspiciously.

Because I hacked into his GPS as soon as we started moving. By the way, there's no driver up front. The vehicle is driven by computer.

Or maybe by a drone operator located at the Pentagon. I can't be sure.

The vehicle entered an underground garage in the Pentagon and drove around a few minutes before it came to a stop. It was exactly the right time. The door opened and the voice said. "I hope you enjoyed the donuts. They're really delicious. Please follow the light path to the proper portal. Good luck on your evaluation."

"Thank you. You're correct. I really liked the donuts."

What is wrong with you, Josh?" I asked in an annoyed tone. *Why are you talking to a computer?*

Just keeping up with the charade. Maybe it was a drone operator and not a computer, Joshua replied. *You never know.*

We followed the blinking yellow arrows that guided us to one of several doors leading into the building. Another computer or maybe another drone operator, asked Joshua to look into the retina scanner next to the door. The voice was a pleasant woman's voice There was a soft chiming sound indicating he had passed the scan but the door didn't open. "Welcome, Master Sergeant Brown. Please place your right hand on the scanner located under the retina scanner."

There was another soft chime and the voice said as the door— referred to as Portal 7—slid open. "Your Identity has been confirmed. Please follow the blinking red arrows that take you to your evaluation room. Good luck on your evaluation."

Don't say anything to it, I thought. *Once was enough.*

The blinking red arrows took us down a long silent hallway with mysterious lightening. As we walked, ceiling lights came on directly above us and about thirty feet further down the hallway. After a few minutes of walking we stopped, turned and looked behind us. The hallway behind us was in complete darkness as if it never existed. The silence was complete. There were no sounds in the hallway or coming from any of the many doorways we passed. Joshua thought to me as we continued following the blinking red arrows, *This reminds me of a scene from one of the* Halloween *movies.*

I was thinking of The Texas Chainsaw Massacre, I replied.

A few minutes later we arrived at our door. Another retina scan and the door slid silently open and we walked into a small room with a single desk and chair. On the table was a lap top computer with the blinking message: **Welcome Marine Master Sergeant Joshua Brown. Please touch any key to begin your evaluation process.**

Joshua sat down at the desk and touched the Enter button. The door behind us slid silently closed as the screen on the laptop displayed a message scrolling downward. The first command was: **If English is your first language, Please touch 1. If not, touch 2.**

Joshua touched the 1 button and the scroll continued. A man's deep baritone voice read the message aloud as it scrolled. I assumed that was for people who couldn't read or maybe for a blind person. Who knew?

The resonant baritone voice began, "Welcome to the written part of your evaluation. You are required to finish each section of the written evaluation before moving on to the next section. There are a total of six sections and you must complete each section within one hour from the time the evaluation begins. You are allowed a thirty-minute break at the end of the third section. Lunch will be provided for you at that time.

"This written evaluation is aimed at determining several specific objective such as intelligence, family history, personal traits and preferences and honesty to name a few. We will use this information to determine your suitability for potential assignments.

"Once the written part of your evaluation is completed you will move on to the physical part of the evaluation which will be conducted at other venues. In all, the total evaluation process will take between three to five days. Good luck Master Sergeant Joshua Brown."

The scroll stopped and another blinking message appeared on the laptop screen: **When you are ready to begin your first section of the written evaluation, please touch the 1 key. If you need a bathroom**

break before beginning, touch the 2 key, you will be granted a 15-minute delay.

We both thought the same simultaneously, *Touch the 2 key.*

"You are granted a 15-minute delay. Counting down now." A clock appeared on the display counting down as a door on the right wall I had not noticed slid open revealing a bathroom.

This is the weirdest thing I've ever heard of, I thought to Joshua. *Do you want to continue this?*

Absolutely yes! he replied as he did his business at the urinal. *It maybe my only chance of appearing in a James Bond movie or something like it. If I change my mind are you sure we can get out of here? The security seems pretty tight.*

Stick with me, bro. I can get us out of here in a heartbeat.

Really? He sounded skeptical. *Are you sure?*

Pretty sure, I replied. *I'll know more once I see how the evaluations go.*

We returned to the desk with the clock showing 4:57 left on the countdown. Joshua hit the Enter button and screen updated.

The baritone voice was back, "Welcome to the first section of your evaluation. You have sixty minutes from the time you start. You must answer every question as honestly as you can. Please consider your answer to each question carefully. You are allowed to change your answers at any time within the hour, but once the hour is up changes are no longer permitted. Pauses within the hour once the evaluation begins are not permitted. Please touch the Enter button to continue to the first section of your evaluation."

Joshua took a deep breath and touched the Enter button. The following questionnaire appeared:

Written Evaluation Section 1

Assuming you are currently or have recently served in the military, as a police officer or a government agent:

1. Have you ever killed anyone in combat? Yes or No
2. If your answer to 1 is yes, please indicate how many you have killed in combat

a. 1-5
b. 6-10
c. Not sure how many
d. More than I can count

3. How did you feel about killing combatants?

a. It made me sick
b. Very bad
c. I got used to it
d. I enjoyed killing them

4. Have you ever killed any non-combatants?
5. If your answer to 4 is yes, please indicate how many non-combatants have you killed

a. 1-5
b. 6-10
c. Not sure how many
d. More than I can count

6. How do you feel about killing non-combatants?

a. It was an accident
b. It made me sad
c. It didn't bother me
d. Some people need to die

7. If you had to kill someone, what would be your weapon of choice?

a. My bare hands
b. With a knife
c. With a pistol at short range
d. With a rifle as far away as possible
e. Bombs or rockets so I don't have to see

    f. It depends on the situation

  8. If you were ordered to kill one or many people by your superior, what would you do?

    a. Refuse

    b. Refuse unless justified

    c. Require a written order

    d. Kill them as ordered

  9. Have you ever enjoyed killing someone? Yes or No

  10. Have you ever regretted killing someone? Yes or No

Joshua and I were stunned by the questionnaire. Why on Earth would they be asking these questions? What possible reason could they have other than they were looking for candidates to become assassins.

It took us the full hour to decide how to answer all ten questions. We wanted to be honest but we didn't want to come off as some kind of psychopath. During our time in the Marines we had killed a number of people, mostly in situations where it was kill or be killed. Unfortunately, there were a few cases of collateral damage, which we grieved over for a very long time. I think it is best summed up in the answers to questions 9 and 10.

Question 9: Did you ever enjoy killing someone? Enjoy is definitely too strong of a word but I was definitely glad I was able to kill Taliban soldiers who used women and children as shields to hide behind while they killed our troops.

Question 10: Did you ever regret killing someone? It sickened me every time one of those human shields died because I missed the shot at the enemy and killed the shield instead. Both Joshua and I still grieve for those who died because we weren't able to kill the intended target.

The bottom line was we answered 'yes' to both questions 9 and 10.

The next sections were easy by comparison. We breezed through the next two sections that dealt with questions about our history, from our youngest memories to present day. Of course, we felt obligated to leave out anything about my spirit life and being bonded to Joshua. We were sure that might have them rethink returning Josh to the VA hospital and the Loony Tunes ward.

Section 2 dealt with family issues. Did you have both a father and mother growing up? Did you love your parents? Did they ever abuse you? Were they strict with you? How did you get along with your twin brother? Those type of questions.

Section 3 covered our education. Did you like school? Did you get good grades? What were your favorite subjects? Where there any subjects you truly disliked? What about school sports? What was your favorite? Were you good at sports. When was your first kiss? How old were you when you first had sex? What are your sexual preferences? And on and on *ad nauseum*.

Many may notice, I'm not supplying answers to the above questions. Joshua answered all of the questions truthfully as required. That doesn't mean he intended to share that information with anyone else who may be reading our memoirs. And I agreed whole heartedly (metaphorically speaking, of course).

When Joshua had supplied the last answer to Section 3, the computer displayed the message that it was time for a lunch break and the countdown clock image appeared, counting backwards from 30 minutes. At the same moment an invisible shelf next to the invisible bathroom door slid out and a soft chime sounded notifying his lunch was waiting. Joshua stood up and headed for the shelf and stopped halfway there. *How did they know?* he thought to me.

Since I wasn't going to be eating, I continued focusing on the last few questions we'd discussed until Joshua thought to me, *Look, Caleb. My favorite lunch. Steak and Shake prime Steakburger combo with a chocolate milkshake and a Coke Zero chaser. How did they know what I'd like?*

After all the evaluation questions, I replied, *they know everything about you. If they know all about your sex life, I'm sure they know what you want for lunch.*

The thirty minutes passed quickly but my boy is a speed eater and finished his lunch in fifteen. He used the bathroom and washed the remnants of his steak burger off his face and waited for the rest of the evaluation sections.

Section 4 was a standard IQ test. I always thought they were over rated. They don't really measure intelligence; they just determine how much you know. They aren't the same thing. You can know a lot of useless facts, which is what the IQ test measures. It doesn't measure how you can look at all these facts and decide how to integrate the important stuff into something useful. I think there should be a knowledge test and a separate wisdom test which measures if you can make wise decisions based on your knowledge. Since nobody ever asked me my opinion, we were stuck with the IQ test.

Between Joshua and myself, I felt he did very well on the section. We were able to answer at least eighty percent of the questions quickly. For the other twenty percent, after discussing it between ourselves, we were pretty confident in some of our answers. The last ten percent, neither of us had a clue. Fortunately, as a spirit with special inhuman abilities, I may or may not have accessed the internet to aid in arriving at the correct answer. Joshua knows nothing about my unsanctioned information search. Mum's the word.

Section 5 was an evaluation of ethical practices as they pertain to armed conflicts. I believed its purpose was to measure how we determine the limits of our behavior during war time with both enemy combatants and civilians. This was tough but we pretty much agreed with our Rules of Engagement. Every mission had their own ROEs established by our superiors. We could ask for clarification prior to the beginning of a mission and even ask for modifications during a mission if things started going sideways but we didn't remember ever ignoring the ROEs. We based his answers on this approach.

Section 6 was titled Scenarios. We were given six ten-minute sessions to determine plans for how to best meet our mission objectives. This was right up our alley. Both of us had been master sergeants in a Marine Corps recon battalion. This is what we did every day for several years when we were in Afghanistan. We were given mission objectives for our squads to complete. Our job was to determine the best way to meet the objectives with the troops we had. The mission always came first, the safety of our men and women troops came next. Initially, we were put in command of squads of nine or ten Marines. Later we were responsible for platoons of three or four squads. We were very good at what we did.

It began with simple straight forward missions and built to very complicated missions but nothing we hadn't experienced during our tours of duty. I believe we addressed all the questions correctly.

When the hour was up, we expected to see something on the computer screen like: "Your Written Evaluation has been successfully completed. Thank you for your participation. You will receive feedback on your performance within 24 hours. Have a pleasant evening. We look forward to seeing you tomorrow to begin the second phase of your evaluation."

Instead, the message read: **Please remain seated. Another Section has been added to your evaluation. Section 7 will be an extension of Section 6 with the exception that you will need to adjust your battle plan while the mission is in progress due to unexpected intel regarding the enemy. Your mission goals will remain the same.** A second or two passed and the voice said, "The following is your mission: A Taliban platoon has captured a small village of about a hundred locals just west of Kabul. The Taliban platoon has been cut off from their supply line and are using the locals as hostages until reinforcements arrive. Those reinforcements are expected to arrive within thirty minutes.

"Your mission is to recapture the village with minimum casualties to the locals. Your platoon is ordered to kill or capture all of the Taliban troops. Your success will be measured by the number of locals you save.

"The Taliban platoon is located on the south side of the village. The reinforcements are expected to come from the north. You have fifteen minutes to brief your troops on your battle plan before the scenario begins. Unlike the previous sections this section will be done in a virtual reality environment. Goggles and weapons will be supplied at the end of this introduction. This introduction has ended."

"Holy shit! Are you kidding me?" Joshua, screamed out loud but I was thinking the same thing.

These people haven't been doing their homework. Which of the Marines in our battalion had the highest score in the virtual reality game Call of Duty? Joshua thought to me.

If I remember correctly, it was me, I answered.

No it wasn't. It was me or maybe we were tied, Joshua countered. *Anyway this is going to be fun.*

Not so fast. I got a bad feeling this is going to be like the Kobayashi Maru *episode on Star Trek. The only way you can win is by cheating."*

You got a problem with that, Caleb? You already set the precedent by accessing the internet to get IQ test answers if I remember correctly.

You're right, Josh. Get ready to show them what we've got.

We had fifteen minutes to arm our platoon. I called up the list of weapons available as Joshua looked at the computer screen.

What I want is a way of knocking everyone unconscious without killing them, Joshua said. *Are mortars or grenades on the list of weapons?*

Both are on the list but only the explosive types, I replied.

Can you use your magic powers to change them from the explosives to sleeping gas containers?

Maybe, I answered. *Let me give it a try.*

A few minutes later I figured out how to modify the explosives to sleeping gas. I also double checked the list of other equipment to see if gas masks were on the list but found none.

Joshua had a good question. *Will whoever is playing against me be able to see the changes you made?*

I'm pretty sure you are going to be playing against a computer. I don't get any indication they are aware of my modifications.

Joshua smiled broadly and thought to me, *Then let's arm our platoon and get this party started.*

All of our platoon was spread out and hidden by burned out cars and trucks, the rubble of partially destroyed buildings and behind a large fountain in the middle of the village. When the 'game' began our people began tossing gas grenades and firing gas filled mortars as quickly as they could.

Whoever/whatever was controlling the Taliban was totally caught by surprise. The bad guys were only able to fire a few harmless shots before they were overcome by the sleeping gas. Our own troops were far enough away from the gas they weren't affected. They waited a few minutes for the gas to clear and moved in to capture the Taliban and make sure the locals were taken care of. We completed our mission in less than fifteen minutes.

Joshua removed his VR visor and looked at the computer screen. A note scrolled across the monitor. It was read by the deep baritone voice, "Congratulations on your victory. However your victory is forfeited because you cheated."

"I didn't cheat," said Joshua in his deeper bass voice. "I was innovative. If you had constructed your software so it couldn't be adjusted, it might have been a different outcome. But I won fair and square."

There was a long pause before the baritone replied, "This completes your first day of evaluation. You will be returned to your hotel and tomorrow you will be contacted regarding your physical evaluation."

The door behind us slid open and we followed the red blinking arrows to our autonomously driven vehicle which returned us to the hotel. It had been a very interesting day. We couldn't wait for the next challenge.

CHAPTER 13

Let the Games Begin—Joshua

When we arrived back at our hotel, I was feeling pretty good about how the first day of evaluations had gone. Caleb agreed but he seemed uneasy. I asked him why.

He answered, *It bothers me we didn't see any other people. Do you think you could have been the only person being evaluated? Like maybe they already have in mind some special mission for you to lead? It seems strange they didn't have a room full of people undergoing the evaluations at the same time. It's hardly cost effective to have each person evaluated separately. I was also uncomfortable we didn't see a single person who might have been involved in conducting your evaluation. I think everything was done by computers. Don't you think that was kind of spooky?*

I hadn't given it much thought but Caleb was right. It *was* kind of spooky. Not that I think our government, or at least the military part of our government, is above spending huge amounts of money on trivial things, five-hundred dollar hammers and toilets costing thousands of dollars come to mind.

Another concern came to mind: since the evaluation was being held in the Pentagon, we assumed it was a military funded mission but maybe one of the other agencies was 'renting' the Pentagon facilities for the evaluations. Based on the close-to-the-vest operations of the alphabet agencies (CIA, FBI, DEA, NSA, DHS, *ad infinitum*) the military may not have any idea what's going on.

Knowing Caleb and his new found abilities to use the computer, I was pretty sure he was going to try to hack our government agencies' secure websites to dig for answers to our concerns while I slept.

Joshua, wake up. We need to talk.

I had been sound asleep but the tone of his message woke me instantly. Without moving, I opened my eyes and found the room totally black. It was still night time. Reflexively, I slowly reached under my pillow and got hold of my Auto Mag and pulled it silently down to my side, clicking off the safety. *Attack?* I thought to him.

No. You don't need your weapon. Something is going down I don't understand. Just listen. Okay?

Okay, I replied. *What's up?*

I've been searching the web since you went to sleep and I can't find anything regarding this evaluation you're undergoing. I can't find any record that you ever received any orders to report for the test or any test results. I've searched everything I could think of and came up empty. That includes the dark web.

I expanded my search and couldn't find any reference to either you or me. We don't show up in any of the Marine records that we ever joined the Corps or served in Afghanistan. The VA hospital in Atlanta has no record of you being admitted or escaping. There is nothing in the University of Mississippi data bases that you were ever on the staff of their athletic department nor could I find any record of you attending the Krav Maga seminars. The YouTube video of you demonstrating Krav Maga blocking techniques is no longer available nor any record it ever existed.

What's going on, Caleb? How can this be happening? I interrupted.

Wait, bro. There's more, he replied.

There's no record we attended high school. I checked out the online version of our year books and we are no longer in them. The scariest bit of information is that there are no longer any records of our birth or the birth and death of our parents. For all intents and purposes we never existed.

Why would anyone do this to us? I asked, incredulously. *Who would do such a thing to us?*

Only our government has the ability to completely wipe out all those records. I can think of only one reason why they went to all that trouble. They want to turn you into a superspy, known only to very few people at the highest level of our government. Oh, by the way, we're no longer registered at this hotel anymore and there's no record you ever checked in. The record says the room is not occupied and hasn't been for several days. It's showing up as being remodeled.

There was a very long silence as I processed what my brother just revealed to me. That was a lot of shit dumped on me in the middle of the night. After what must have seemed like an eternity to Caleb, I replied to him, *Let's play this out. But we need to be very careful. The alternative to superspy could be they want to get rid of me and are just preparing the record to say I never existed in the first place.*

Good plan, bro, Caleb thought back to me. *One of the things I love about you is that you never back down from a challenge. And this is going to be the challenge of a lifetime.*

<u>Time for Round Two (Maybe)—Caleb</u>

Bright and early the next morning, we received an encrypted message on the lap top.

> **To:** Marine Master Sergeant Joshua Brown
> **Re:** Physical Evaluation
>
> You are ordered to begin your physical evaluation this morning at 0900 hours. Transport will pick you up in front of your hotel at 0800 hours to be delivered to the site where your evaluation will be conducted. Bring all workout gear and any weapons you consider necessary for this evaluation. Please confirm your receipt of this message.

I immediately sent a reply as requested by Joshua.

Reply: I cannot comply with the above order because, according to US Marine Corps records, Master Sergeant Joshua Brown never existed, neither did his brother or their parents. If you feel there has been some error in the US Marine Corps records, please feel free to contact this non-existent person at your earliest convenience.

We waited in our room, the room that was supposed to be undergoing renovation. We continued to wait until well after 0800 hours. At 0915 hours the hotel phone rang. We ignored it. It rang twice more during the morning and once in the afternoon. At 1300 hours, there was a knock on our door.

Joshua checked through the peep hole in the door and saw a man dressed in a suit and tie who looked unsurprisingly like a Marine out of uniform. Joshua didn't open the door or say anything.

The man knocked again and this time said, "Please open the door, Mr. Brown. It's urgent that I speak with you."

Joshua did not open the door but replied, "This room isn't occupied at the present time. According to hotel records it is being renovated. There are no records of a Mr. Brown checking in to this room or any other room in the hotel."

The man seemed annoyed at Joshua's comments and said through the door, "You don't realize who you are messing with. Open the door immediately or I will be forced to..."

"You don't realize you are shouting at a man who, according to your records, never existed. That makes you a complete fool. Either you admit to screwing up or this conversation is over."

The man turned and headed back to the elevator without further discussion.

I followed him down the hall until the man entered the elevator and spoke on his cell phone. "He refuses to let me in or to even acknowledge he's Brown. Do you want me to breach the door and subdue him?"

Before the person on the other end of the line could answer, I was able to disconnect his call and then deactivate his phone. I returned to our room, informing Joshua of my elevator activities. We were determined to wait it out.

An hour went by, then two. Several threatening messages came and went on the encrypted lap top which we ignored. At the end of a three hour wait, a message appeared that wasn't encrypted.

The message read:

> Congratulations, Mr. Brown. You have successfully completed your evaluation. You exceeded all expectations and we would like to discuss opportunities you may or may not be interested in. All general information about you and your family has been restored. Specific information regarding your

activities as a Marine have been restored but are classified as top secret and available to only a few select individuals on an Eyes Only basis. That includes all data gathered during your written evaluation sessions yesterday.

If you are interested in pursuing your options with us, please let me know by replying to this message. If you decide to pursue other options, you are free to leave at any time you find convenient. Just a few more things. First, our computer techs would love to know how you were able to hack into the *Call of Duty* scenario, modify it and not leave any trace. Second, how were you able to jam our agent's cell phone in the elevator. You don't have to reveal your methods, they're just curiosities as far as I'm concerned.

Hope to hear from you soon regardless of your decision.

The Messenger

Time to Fish or Cut Bait—Joshua

I arranged for a meeting with the Messenger for early the next morning. It had to be someplace public but not so public others could hear our conversation. I decided on the lobby bar at ten in the morning. Not many people were at the bar that early.

I arrived at the bar at 0900 hours and made the call to the Messenger, just to make sure he didn't have time to bug the place. It was to be only the Messenger and me (and Caleb, of course). I chose to sit in the far corner of the bar with a view of the hotel lobby.

Promptly at 1000 hours, a man in a business suit walked into the bar. The bar didn't open until 1100 hours but a substantial tip to the only bartender ensured we had the whole place to ourselves.

I stood and introduced myself and gestured to a seat directly across from me. I was wearing a pair of dockers with a XXXL polo shirt with short sleeves. I wanted to appear intimidating and not happy with the way I had been treated. I gave him my best scowl and waited for him to begin the conversation.

He ignored my scowl and didn't seem to be intimidated by my massive biceps, which hurt my feelings a little. He spoke in a friendly tone of voice and looked me straight in the eyes during our entire conversation. "Mr. Brown, I believe in being direct so I will get right to the point. Everything that happened to you the last few days was done for a purpose. I don't apologize for our methods; I believe they were necessary to evaluate you for a specific series of missions. You were the only candidate and I'm very happy to inform you truly exceeded all of our expectations.

"As of this date, you are no longer on active duty with the Marine Corps. That is why I addressed you as Mr. Brown and will continue to do so. First question; is that a problem for you?"

I dropped the scowl and answered, "No, it doesn't bother me at all. May I ask you a question in return?"

He nodded and answered, "Absolutely, ask me all the questions you want."

"How do I address you? Should I call you sir or do you have a code name or should I continue to refer to you as the Messenger?"

He smiled, it was a friendly smile. "You definitely don't have to call me sir. For now, my code name is Apostle."

"A bible word for messenger, I like that. Next question. If I'm no longer a Marine, which government agency would I be working for if I accept your offer?"

"Excellent question, with a complex answer," the Apostle answered. "Actually, you would be working for all of the alphabet agencies but not all at once. It would depend on what mission you would be handling. One might involve the FBI or DEA, another the CIA or it could be all of them. I would be acting as your go between for whoever is funding your work and supplying your support. However, let me be very clear; you will be the lead on every mission assigned to you. That's the best answer I can give you at this point. Next question?"

"Can you give me some idea as to what type of missions I would be dealing with?" I asked.

"Bingo! That's the real question, isn't it? Unfortunately, I can only give you a limited answer at this time. You have to be all in before I can give you all the details. The following is all that I can tell you. Certain high-level people in our government are frustrated by various laws dealing with really bad people. People like drug cartel bosses, people dealing in human trafficking, and large criminal organizations are a few examples. These people are responsible for much of the crime in our country and they seem to be untouchable. We would want you to touch them. Touch them in a way our established agencies and police cannot. You wouldn't be constrained by federal or local laws. Each mission statement would expressly describe the desired outcome. You would be free to determine the best way for that to happen."

I was a little surprised as to where this was leading. "Are you saying you want me to become an assassin?"

Without hesitation, the Apostle answered, "In some instances the answer would be yes." He paused for a few moments before continuing, then said, "I think of it more as a war then assassination. Your war would be a war on crime with surgical strikes on specific targets. Similar to the hunt for Bin Laden. He was the leader of a terrorist organization who was targeted for assassination along with anyone else who was trying to protect him.

"Your missions would be broader then military targets but I see them as being just as necessary. Not all of your missions would be above the law; I would think any killing you do would be in self-defense as you accomplish your mission."

I sat quietly, actually conversing with Caleb to get his take on all this. The bottom line was we both felt this was a worthwhile endeavor.

"If I sign up, what happens next?" I asked.

"There will be at least six months of training by experts in all types of areas. The training will involve classroom work like learning foreign languages and mission planning. Of course there will be a lot of physical training as well, such as hand to hand combat techniques, all type of weapons training from knives and clubs, sticks and bats, of course every type of firearm you can think of, explosives and that's just a taste.

"After training, there will be a series of missions, each one more complicated than the last. If those go well you will be considered a full-fledged agent."

"How many agents are currently involved in this war on crime?"

"If you accept, you'll be the first one."

"How long do I have to decide?" I asked.

"Until the end of this meeting," the Apostle answered.

I smiled at him and said, "You seem pretty sure of yourself. What if I need more time?"

"Do you need more time?"

I shook my head. "No. You had me at 'war on crime.' I'm in. When do I leave for training?"

"Tomorrow at 1300 hours. When you get back to your room your laptop will have your itinerary and plane ticket waiting for you. I will be your single point of contact throughout your training as well as your missions. When you return to your room there will be a package waiting for you that includes a secure phone to be used only to contact me."

"You seem very sure I would accept your offer to have all that stuff delivered to my room. Are you always so sure of yourself?" I asked.

He smiled again, not a cocky smile, a warm, friendly smile and said, "It's my job to read people, Joshua. I did extensive research on you and the terrible tragedy that happened to your brother. It's in your bloodline from your father on down to you and your brother. You're all patriots. I was sure you would accept the moment you stopped accepting the outlandish steps you were being forced to make.

"If you run into any problems, call me before you contact anyone else. There are only six people in our federal government who know about you or your missions. If you are successful additional agents will be selected and trained and the number of federal people involved will grow along with them but we intend to keep it to a bare minimum. A lot is riding on your success but I have every confidence you will succeed. Good hunting Jacob, I know your brother Caleb would be proud of you."

CHAPTER 14

Beginning of Training at Camp LeJeune—Joshua

We checked out of our fancy hotel the next day and caught a real cab to Washington Ronald Reagan National Airport. I believe that earns an award for the longest name of any airport in America, maybe in the world. I had checked the training schedule and was somewhat surprised I was heading back to Marine Corps Base Camp Lejeune in North Carolina.

For those of you who aren't familiar with the Marine Corps training facilities, let me give you a short tutorial. When a recruit signs up to be a Marine he first goes to basic training. There are two locations for basic, one in Paris Island, South Carolina, the other in San Diego, California. Caleb and I went through the twelve-week program at Paris Island. We went in as recruits and three months later we were officially Marines. Were we ready for combat? Hell no! We knew how to wear the uniform and march in rank and file. We were in much better physical condition than when we arrived at Paris Island and we knew which end of a weapon to point at the enemy but by no means were we ready to fight a war. That training came later at a different location.

After a weekend pass to see our family, we were sent to Marine Corps Base Camp LeJeune in North Carolina about 250 miles north of Paris Island. Camp LeJeune was huge, 153,439 acres huge, larger than the entire state of Rhode Island. It was there where we were turned into battle ready Marines.

The camp hosts numerous training activities. I won't go into what they are except for what Caleb and I went through. We were assigned to the School of Infantry, which was divided into two sections, the Infantry Training Battalion (ITB) and Marine Combat Training (MCT).

Caleb and I were assigned to the ITB where we underwent extensive training on how to effectively use a wide variety of personal weapons, including knives, fists, feet and anything handy (garbage can lids and baseball bats come to mind).

When we had finished that training, it was 'strongly suggested' Caleb and I volunteer for Reconnaissance Training also referred to as nine weeks in hell.

Recon Marines bear a similarity to Army Rangers, Navy Seals and other Special Forces operations. The training dropout rate is staggering. A few quit, however many are injured and cannot complete the training. Those who survive are considered elite troops. Caleb and I managed to survive but it took several weeks before we quit hurting.

These elite troops adapted a portion of the 23rd Psalm as their motto during the Vietnam War:

Yea Though I Walk Through the Valley of the Shadow of Death

I Will Fear No Evil

For I Am the Meanest Son of a Bitch in the Valley

I think that pretty much sums up how prepared I felt going into this new assignment. Boy, was I overly optimistic.

Back to the Future—Joshua

No more nostalgia. That was almost six years ago. I was no longer a Marine on active duty. I wasn't wearing a uniform and I was treated as a guest agent from some unspecified government agency.

At the check-in desk, I handed my orders to a Marine clerk and she had me take a seat and wait. I was expecting it to be a substantial wait so I put in an air bud and turned on my MP3 player and began listening to an Ace Atkins audio book about Sheriff Quinn Colson in Jericho, Mississippi. I closed my eyes and listened to the beginning of the story.

Ten minutes later, Caleb interrupted, *Heads up, Josh. You got a two-star heading your way.*

I opened my eyes and shut off the audio player. As the general walked up to me, I stood up quickly and came to a ridged attention. The general stopped in front of me, smiled and extended his hand. "Once a Marine, always a Marine," he said casually. "Stand easy, Mr. Brown. I just wanted to personally welcome you back to Camp LeJeune. Would you please accompany me to my office?"

"Lead the way, General."

As we walked down the hallway to his office, I noticed every person in uniform stepped out of the way and remained at attention until we had passed, the general nodding at each of his Marines. To Marines, generals weren't God but they were treated like they were one step below Jesus. I remembered those days and was deathly afraid of any one with stars on their collar.

When we got to the general's office, I was surprised to see the Apostle sitting in one of the comfortable chairs next to the general's spacious desk. To enlisted Marines, a general's office was frequently referred to as 'Heaven.'

The Apostle rose and shook my hand as the general said, "This man doesn't exist and he isn't in my office. In a few minutes you and the non-existent man may or may not be using my secure conference room to discuss matters I am not cleared to know about."

With that said, the general walked to his desk, took a seat and appeared to think we were no longer there. The Apostle gestured to the conference room door. He turned and said to the general, "Thank you General for the use of your facility."

The general continued to ignore us as we entered the conference room but I thought I detected a hint of a smile and he focused on a report he was supposed to be reading.

Let's Get Down to the Real Nitty Gritty—Caleb

It was a small conference room, with six very comfortable chairs encircling a round table. There was a credenza against one wall loaded with a water pitcher, coffee pot, fruit juices and sodas with crystal glasses and china cups and small plates. Next to the drinks was a silver platter with a variety of delicious looking pastries. Next to the pastries were folded linen napkins and silver spoons and forks. I thought about the old adage, 'It's good to be king' and generals and admirals were the kings of the military.

Joshua waited to see what the Apostle did but as soon as he headed for the snack bar, so did my brother. They took seats with full plates and cups of coffee. The room had no windows, secured rooms seldom do. I was pretty sure the room had been swept for bugs just before we entered the general's office. Most of one wall was a screen that could display information from the rooms air-gapped computer or in our case, the laptop the Apostle had brought with him. Joshua had brought his encrypted laptop as well.

There was no chit chat between them. They ate their snacks and drank their coffee as the Apostle hooked up his lap top to the display screen, powered it up and the first page of the presentation came alive on the screen. By then the snacks were gone and the Apostle began his briefing.

"What I'm about to share with you is above Top Secret. It has no name designation and only a handful of people have access to it and most of them don't know who the others are.

"In general terms, your missions will entail two things: protecting human targets and taking out those who wish to do them harm. Each mission assigned to you will make clear those who are the human targets and who the bad guys are. If the bad guys resist you don't arrest them, local authorities, state police and federal agencies will handle all arrests. If they attack you, you are sanctioned to kill them without any fear of reprisal. If they surrender to you, you are to restrain them and contact the proper agency. This will be a war on crime and the criminals who commit them. Do you have any questions so far?"

During the brief pause, I thought to Joshua, *What if the arresting authorities are dirty and release the bad guys or a judge gets paid off to set them free?*

Joshua asked the question and the Apostle answered, "Your mission isn't over until the bad guys are either dead or in a maximum security federal prison. Anyone who helps the bad guys is your target as well. Good question, any others?"

Joshua shook his head and the Apostle continued, "The main purpose of this meeting is to make you aware of your training agenda. Some of the training will be done by Marine instructors as well as instructors from other government agencies. Before you leave this room, you will be issued a red security badge with your name on it. You must keep that in your possession at all times. That badge will be the only key to your room in the Bachelor Office Quarters. The BOQ houses officers from all of the military services including foreign military personnel. In addition, civilian agencies contract with Camp LeJeune for specialized training with their agents. Those agents also are housed in the BOQ. That would include you. The badge also authorizes you to eat at the officer's club and your meals are all paid for. The same applies to any purchases you need to make at the base commissary and exchange.

"You may be required to attend training functions at other federal agency sites. That is still to be determined. Any other questions before I get to the training agenda?"

Joshua nodded and asked, "Is there any provision for leave during the training?"

"Not at the present time, however, in the case of an emergency we would have to determine each request individually. Anything else?"

Joshua shook his head and the Apostle replied, "Good, let's move on to the training agenda."

He pushed a button on his laptop and a list of training activities was seen. "The training activities are divided into two categories," he said, "class room and field exercises. The class room activities are: Language Training, Mission Planning (Strategic and Tactical), and Logistic Support. Any questions so far?"

Joshua nodded his head and said, "I understand items two and three but why do I need to learn a new language?"

Before the Apostle could answer, I thought to Joshua, *I got that covered, bro. Just chill.*

But then the Apostle said, "You aren't going to learn just one foreign language, you're going to learn six. We already have your first three missions selected and each mission requires you to be fluent in other languages. You don't have to speak like a native but you will need to know certain key phrases. It won't be as difficult as it sounds."

Joshua looked totally stunned! He'd been a slow learner as a child. He didn't start speaking English until he was almost two and only a few people could understand what he was saying. I 'yelled' at him, *Don't panic, Josh. You've got to calm down. It's going to be okay. Trust me on this, it will be one of the easiest parts of your training. I guarantee it. Just stay cool and calm. I'll brief you on it when we get to the BOQ.*

He swallowed hard and gave a slight nod of his head to let me know he was alright. Then he asked, "Okay, what are the field exercises?"

"There are three areas of field exercises. They are: Physical Fitness, Hand to Hand Combat, which I might add will include honing your Krav Maga skills and Weapons Training where you will be introduced to a very wide range of weapons you may never have used before.

"That about wraps up what I have to say about your training agenda. When you leave the conference room, see the general's aide and they will give you your ID badge and a map of where all your training sites will be. Tomorrow you will spend the morning in your first Spanish class. In the afternoon, you will meet with your physical fitness instructors in the Strength and Conditioning Facility. When it's time to move on to other training you will be given twenty four hours' notice. It will be sent to your encrypted laptop. Make sure you secure the laptop in the safe in your bedroom closet. If you lose your laptop or badge you're in deep doodoo. You have my secured email address, use it if you need to get in touch with me."

He stood and offered his hand. I shook it and thanked him for the information. "Good luck to you, Mr. Brown. I wish you all the luck in the world. You're going to need it."

I followed them out of the conference room and noticed the general had left his office. Joshua met with the general's aide who gave him his badge and the map of the training facility. It hadn't changed much in the six years we had been away.

He was picked up in an electric cart outside the base headquarters and driven to the BOQ where he unpacked his duffel and got settled in. The next order of business was for me to explain how I was going to magically transform him into being multilingual. I couldn't wait.

It's Great To Be Home Again / Maybe Not—Caleb

Most of all the training we had done previously in the Marines was done in groups, both small and large. All of Joshua's training at Camp LeJeune was done alone. Well, not quite alone. He always had a team of instructors showing him how to do almost everything better than he ever imagined. And of course, I was there to help whenever I could.

Not everything was physically demanding, although most of it was. Learning a new foreign language wasn't physically demanding but it could be emotionally draining. Learning one language was bad enough, unfortunately, he was expected to learn to speak six:

Spanish
Russian
Japanese
Chinese (both Mandarin and Cantonese)
Arabic

For the first few days, he spent four hours every morning struggling with Spanish. He was immersed with several native Spanish speakers. He hated it. By the afternoon, he had a massive headache. I let it go on just so he would be ready to accept my help.

Language instructors were brought in to tutor Joshua from the very prestigious Defense Language Institute Foreign Language Center based at the Presidio of Monterey in California. The language classes at DLIFLC normally run from 36 weeks to 64 weeks based on difficulty of the language being learned. The last four languages listed above were considered to be in the 64-week training category. Joshua didn't have 64 weeks. He had 26 weeks to learn them all. What were they to do? Their plan was to use newly developed crash course techniques. Well, not exactly true.

Way back in the day they tried hypnotizing people and putting them into a trance and playing language tapes while they were supposedly resting during the trance state. This technique met with very limited success. Then they tried a variety of drug cocktails to enhance the rate of programming the mind with a new language, with pretty much the same results. I wasn't sure what they were going to try but the last thing I wanted was for them to start using drugs like sodium pentothal and him blabbing about his spirit brother.

Fortunately, I was able to assist with the languages. When using telepathy to communicate with each other, we speak what I call a universal language. If I wanted to communicate telepathically to a native Japanese speaker for example, they would have no problem understanding what I 'said' even though I don't speak a word of Japanese (well maybe a few words I picked up during karate class). And the reverse was also true. When they spoke to me in Japanese, I would tap into their minds and 'hear' the universal language. No *problemo.*

I know this is going to sound ridiculous but it was relatively easy for me to program Joshua's mind when he was asleep to think the words in English and permit him to say them in whichever foreign language he needed to speak. With the permission of my spirit teacher, I was allowed to program Joshua's mind, a little bit each day so not to make it look like he was possessed by a language demon. By the end of two weeks he spoke Spanish fluently.

His teachers were amazed at how quickly he learned and how clearly he spoke without a hint of accent. Some thought he had at least some Spanish classes while he was in high school. However, when they checked with his school they discovered they didn't offer any foreign languages while Joshua attended. "It's truly a miracle," one of the instructors said. Another replied, "I've never seen anyone pick up a new language so completely. He even understands the idioms."

To make it seem more difficult, I stretched Joshua's programming out to six weeks when he started Mandarin and nine weeks for Cantonese. I also input a few errors in his translations to make him appear more human. His instructors still praised his accomplishments however they were more subdued. He finished all his language training in a total of 23 weeks. I was very proud of him. My brother the linguist!

CHAPTER 15

Nostalgia Strikes Again—Joshua

Strength and conditioning were always something I enjoyed. Even before Caleb and I started high school, we were always pushing each other to get stronger and bigger but also faster and more flexible.

When we were twelve we found some old books on physical fitness and how you didn't need any weights to stay in shape. That was a good thing since my family didn't have the money to join a gym or even to buy a few dumbbells. Instead of lifting weights we started doing chin-ups, sit-ups and push-ups and other body weight exercises. When those became too easy, we'd take turns sitting on each other while one of us did push-ups or holding heavy stuff against our chests as we did the sit-ups.

We'd go to the park whenever we had some free time (which wasn't much due to the chores our mama had us doing). We'd race each other up and down the walking paths through the park. We didn't have any bikes so we ran everywhere we went.

By the time we got into high school we were a little over six feet tall. We thought we were pretty muscular until we saw some of the upperclassmen. I remember Caleb saying to me the first day of our freshmen year, "I want to look like that."

Our high school had a really big weight room and there were two PE teachers who wouldn't let you touch a weight until they showed you how not to hurt yourself when you were lifting. Both of the teachers were huge and exceptionally strong.

All freshmen and sophomore students were required to take a PE class every day. There were a variety of exercise classes, even intramural games like ping pong and volleyball but if you tried out for interscholastic sports (football, baseball, track, basketball and wrestling come to mind) you were required to do weight training at least part of the year. Once your sport was in season the weight training was limited. You spent most of your time learning how to play your sport.

Caleb and I really enjoyed the weight training in the off seasons. One of our PE teachers put together power lifting contests and my brother and I were the first to sign up. He'd track all our performance records, recording everybody's best lifts. By our senior year we we're the biggest and strongest dudes in the school and won several power lifting tournaments outside of school. By then we were 6'-5" and weighed around 300 pounds.

When we enlisted in the Marines, we continued to dominate all the strength training the Marines had to offer, with the exception of our drill instructors. Some of our DIs made us look like we'd never lifted a weight before. Even a few of the female Drill Instructors had incredible strength in their legs and could do sets of leg presses for twenty reps with 500 pounds. Caleb and I could do more reps with more weight but not very much more. The male DIs kept referring to the weight the new recruits managed to lift as 'pussy weight.'

One of the women DIs loved to shame the recruits. She was a huge, muscular woman who'd shake her head and look really sad then say, "What's happening to the Marines? Is this the best they can recruit nowadays? These feeble excuses for recruits can't even lift pussy weight. What is the Corps coming to?"

After she had dressed down a few of the smaller recruits she brought out a box of baby rattles and had them do a hundred reps with a rattle in one hand while sucking their thumb on the other hand.

It was amazing to Caleb and I how everyone transformed during those twelve weeks of basic. Sure, we had some dropouts. There are always those who live up to Dirty Harry's famous comment, "A man's gotta know his limitations." Those who made it through were stronger, faster and smarter than when they began. And most important to me was Caleb's comment when we had completed basic and were ready to move on to the next challenge. "It's like we just got a whole lot of brothers, people I'd bet my life on during a dust-up."

We got two weeks leave before we were due at Camp LeJeune. We visited with our mama and papa and you could tell how proud they were of us, especially our pops. For a couple of days Caleb and I exchanged training stories with our dad, comparing how it was back in the day before he went to Vietnam. Mama had to practically pry him away from us in order for him to attend church and Bible study on Wednesdays. Of course we accompanied them. We really liked being back and watching our dad preach his sermons and Mama leading the ladies' Bible study group. She just had to drag us in front of all the ladies and show us off. It was a little embarrassing when some of the ladies began introducing their grown-up daughters to us. They were pretty obvious. Caleb said they should be wearing a sign around their necks saying, Certified Match Maker.

When the two weeks leave was up, it was really tough to say good-bye again. It was a quiet ride on the bus from home to Camp LeJeune, both of us lost in our private thoughts. Just before our bus arrived, Caleb leaned over and asked me, "So which one of the girls from the church do you plan to take to our graduation ceremony?"

Keeping a straight face, I answered, "The prettiest one, of course."

"So sorry, bro. I already asked her," Caleb answered.

"Are you talking about the plump one with one blue eye and one brown one? She looks about your speed."

The bus came to a stop at a gate with a big sign over the entrance. It read: Welcome to Camp LeJeune, Where Marines are Made. We climbed out of the bus, picked up our duffels and walked through the gate to continue our training.

Fitness and conditioning at Camp LeJeune was an order of magnitude tougher compared to Paris Island basic training. It was similar but more intense. It ended with a 50-mile run in full gear which meant carrying a forty-pound pack on your back.

Recon training was more focused on conditioning. I can't go into detail but it was a measure of how much you could endure until you could go no further. I was hoping I didn't have to repeat the final test. I came very close to giving up. The only way Caleb and I got through it was by challenging each other when things got almost unbearable.

When it was over, we were drained, both physically and emotionally. We both slept for 24 hours after the brief ceremony congratulating us on surviving nine weeks of hell. At the end of the ceremony, we were informed we were assigned to the 2nd Reconnaissance Battalion of the 2nd Marine Division. After a short leave, we shipped out to Afghanistan for our first tour.

CHAPTER 16

You Load 16 Tons & What Do You Get? A Sore Back— Joshua

I promise that was the end of nostalgia. Moving on to more of my new training assignments. First up was fitness and conditioning. The Marines strongly embrace the principle of a sound mind and body. To ensure each Marine is up to the physical part of those standards, there is rigorous physical training. Even though I was no longer a Marine on active duty, they were going to make sure I was physically fit.

The first meeting was basically an evaluation of my present condition as compared to what they felt I needed to be mission ready. On one day I would shoot for lifting maximum weight for a single repetition. There were four different lifts required: the bench, the squat, the dead lift and the power clean.

They told me what the minimum acceptable weight was for each lift and you got three attempts to beat the minimum weight goal. Fortunately, my strength training at Ole Miss prepared me well for this evaluation. I exceeded the minimum acceptable amount by at least 30%. The next day they loaded the bar at a relatively lighter weight and I was expected to do as many repetitions a possible. This was beginning to be very similar to what the NFL Combine used to rank potential professional football players. Again, I exceeded the minimum acceptable reps by a substantial margin, however, I was really spent. The next day was for recovery. I spent a lot of time on a massage table in ice baths and hot tubs. The following day was used to measure flexibility. The day after that was to measure my time in a variety of sprints. The sixth day they timed me on several one mile runs with a thirty-minute break between each one. The seventh day I got a day of rest which I really needed. Praise the Lord for the Sabbath.

The first day of the next week I was told I exceeded all the strength and fitness requirements and recommended I continue my training routine for three times a week for at least two hours each session.

I was ecstatic! Two down (counting the language classes) and for more to go.

Hand to Hand Combat, Let's Dance—Caleb

There are seemingly an endless number of hand to hand combat styles, both formal and informal. There are also endless debates on which is the most effective. Joshua would readily agree that I had a slight edge over him when it came to this type of combat. He preferred to use a weapon, any type of weapon, rather than what he called naked fighting. Not that he wasn't adequate when it came to a fight, it was just that he felt it took a lot more work to kill an enemy with his bare hands. He considered it a last resort.

I feel it's important to separate combat from sport. The main difference is sport fighting seldom ends up with someone dying. In combat it's just the opposite. I know that some, perhaps many would say that's not completely accurate. Many styles of the martial arts are based on self-defense; you're taught how to defend yourself from an aggressor. Only a few styles teach you how to *be* the aggressor.

When you're learning any type of martial art, the objective is to learn, not to kill. That mind set leads to developing a set of rules. Rules such as you aren't permitted to gouge out an eye, crush your opponent's testicles or rip out his throat. Strangling is also frowned upon.

It's a small step form having rules to becoming a sport. Don't get me wrong. I'm not against classical martial arts, they're a really good way of protecting yourself. And I enjoyed watching and participating in tournaments. However for a Marine in combat with no weapons but their body parts (i.e. hands, feet, elbows, knees, teeth and forehead) your objective is to kill your enemy as quickly as you can.

If I had to pick a style of martial arts to teach Marines, it would be Krav Maga. Yes, it can be a method of self-defense, however I believe it is most adaptable to being an aggressor. I strongly believe in the three principals taught by Rabbi Gad Dagan:

1.   Be First
2.   Be Fast
3.   Explosive Power

It was my understanding that the US Marine Corps agreed with my assessment. That was why they taught us some of the techniques during our combat training. I wasn't surprised to find out Rabbi Dagan and some of his instructors were selected to work with Joshua.

Of course, I was with Joshua when we met up with the rabbi and his three instructors. There were a lot of handshakes and even a hug or two. "It's such a pleasure to see you again, my boy. So you decided to become a secret agent man and turn down my most generous offer," he said in a teasing tone with a smile on his face.

"No sir," Joshua replied. "I was all set to accept your offer when Uncle Sam stepped in. First, he made me a Marine again, then put me on inactive reserves and assigned me to become the first black James Bond. I really had no choice and I really have very little idea what the government wants me to do except this training."

The rabbi tapped his lips with his index finger, making a shushing sound. "Don't reveal too much to us. All we know is we are happy to see you again and share some of our Krav Maga with you. Why don't you stretch out while I share some information with you. Who knows, after you retire from MI6, maybe you'll come to work for me after all, Mr. Black James Bond."

Joshua was dressed in his workout clothes, sweatpants, T-shirt and barefoot. They were in what looked like a small wrestling room with mats on most of the floor. There were a variety of charts hanging on the walls some showing stretching techniques, others were lists of training records. A set of double doors were closed and locked and another door led to the locker room.

One of the instructors, a woman named Donna Rule, stepped onto the mat and said to Joshua, "Please follow my stretching routine."

Joshua followed her onto the mat and began to copy her first stretch while the rabbi began his introduction. "Krav Maga was created by a Hungarian-Israeli named Imi LIchtenfeld in the 1930s. He was trained as a boxer and wrestler and developed Krav Maga and taught it to the Jewish community to defend themselves against fascist groups in Bratislava.

"The name Krav Maga is Hebrew for contact combat. It is derived from a combination of techniques used in aikido, boxing, judo, karate and wrestling. Its philosophy emphasizes aggression and simultaneous defensive and offensive maneuvers. There are two types of this martial art; one type is used by the Israeli security forces and the other is for civilian use. We will be teaching you the ISF techniques."

Joshua had gone through Donna's stretching routine but she told him to get down on the mat for partner stretching. They faced each other with their legs spread as far apart as they could with their feet touching. She grabbed both of Joshua's hands and leaned back slowly, pulling Joshua towards her until it felt like she was pulling his thigh bones from his hips. Donna's back was almost touching the floor when she said, "Now you pull me" and they reversed position. Except she ended up with her chest on the floor and her head almost buried in his groin. They went back and forth several times and Joshua seemed to be able to stretch further with each rep. When they finished he was able to lay his head on her lap. For some reason he had a smile on his face when they changed positions for the next stretch.

The rabbi added a few more comments, "It's very important that you perfect a simultaneous strategy of defend and attack. When you attack, continue to strike your opponent until they are completely incapacitated. Always target attacks to your opponent's most vulnerable points, such as: eyes, neck or throat, face, solar plexus, groin, ribs, knee, foot, fingers and liver. And remember, use simple and easily repeatable strikes. That's it for now. If Donna is done with your stretching, let's begin training."

I was a little surprised they had Joshua put on protective gear. In fact I was surprised they had gear large enough to fit him. They had him put on head gear, chest and back vest and a groin protector and It was all light weight gear that wouldn't restrict his movements while offering adequate protection. At least I hoped it was adequate. He also wore MMA gloves, kind of like light weight boxing gloves with fingers which permitted him to grab his opponents.

His opponent was a large man named Yuri but not as large as Joshua. My brother had at least fifty pounds on him but he was quick, extremely quick. The rabbi yelled, "Fight!" and Yuri hit Joshua in the nose before he could get his hands up. Blood began to trickle from Josh's nose as the rabbi yelled, "Stop." Then he said, "What's my first rule?"

"Strike first," Joshua answered as Donna shoved what looked like a mini tampon into his right nostril.

"Then why did you not strike first?" The rabbi shook his head and said, "Ready? Fight!"

Again, Yuri made a lightening like strike to Joshua's face but this time he blocked the punch with his left arm while striking Yuri in the face with his right. The punch snapped Yuri's head back and buckled his knees as he staggered back and fought to regain his balance.

Joshua was on him immediately, jabbing him in the face three times before Yuri fell to the mat. Joshua followed him down driving his knee into the man's groin while placing his forearm against Yuri's throat. "Stop!" yelled the rabbi. "That was better. Yuri take a break. Ivan you're up. Let's go again."

And so it went for the better part of an hour, the three instructors taking turns on Joshua. They stopped briefly to repair damage but immediately continued once the flow of blood was cleaned up.

I thought my brother might have a problem fighting against a woman. I was shocked how he showed her no mercy. She had gotten a few strikes and landed a solid hit to his groin which would have taken Josh out if he hadn't been wearing the jock but he really dominated her. She was up for the third time and as soon as the rabbi yelled "Fight," she ran at him screaming like a banshee from hell, jumped up high placing both knees on his shoulders as she brought her elbow down to strike him on the top of his head. Before her elbow made contact, he grabbed both of her legs and pressed her high above his head and slammed her to the mat. She hit so hard she bounced twice before Joshua dropped all of his 300 pounds on top of her body, ready to strike again but the rabbi quickly screamed, "STOP!"

Joshua rolled off of her as Ivan and Yuri ran to her aide. She was unconscious and a quick exam by Yuri indicated she had a concussion. I wasn't aware navy corpsmen were just outside the double doors. They rushed in when Ivan unlocked the doors. They placed her on a gurney and wheeled her out of the room and took her to the Camp LeJeune Navy Hospital.

The rabbi and the two remaining instructors seemed unphased by what had happened to Donna. I couldn't read Joshua's expression but I could feel his sorrow for injuring her.

"Who's up next? Ivan, your turn. Don't hold back."

And they didn't. For a little more than an hour they beat up on each other. The only time they stopped was when the rabbi halted them to show Joshua a new technique to counter some attack he hadn't seen before.

When it was over, the rabbi gave him a summary. "You did well today. Your old training did you well and you quickly picked up the new techniques I showed you. I believe you would benefit from a month of training, three times a week. I want to cover how to deal with attacks with knives, clubs and such. I will tell the Apostle my recommendations. Perhaps you can insert other training on the off days from Krav Maga. How are you feeling?"

"I feel beat up but nothing that won't heal. I appreciate the opportunity to train with you and your instructors," Joshua answered. "I have to admit, I feel bad about what happened to Donna."

"Don't feel bad for Donna," said Yuri. "My wife will recover."

"Your wife?!" exclaimed Joshua. "Oh my God, I'm so…"

"Don't say it. She knew what she was volunteering for. So did we all. She will be so proud to tell our children she was beat up by the Black James Bond."

If I had a mouth, it would have fallen open. What a crazy world we live in. We returned to the BOQ and Joshua took a long shower and went down to the officer's mess for dinner. After he had finished eating, we went over to the Navy Hospital and Joshua paid his respects to Donna who was resting peacefully in her bed. Yuri gave him a sit rep on Donna; she suffered a minor concussion and some bruising but nothing serious. She was going to stay in the hospital overnight but was expected to be released the following day.

Just before we left, Donna said in a soft voice, "Don't feel sorry. Injuries are just part of the training. I'll be fine. I'm glad I had the chance to train with you. Be well, Joshua."

CHAPTER 17

Eeny Meany Miny Moe, What Weapons Do I Need to Go?—Joshua

Weapons training began the next week and was scheduled three afternoons each week for the duration of my training. Its purpose was to familiarize myself with the wide variety of weapons used by the Marines and to ensure I knew how to successfully operate the ones that were the most likely to be in my inventory.

I wasn't limited to only the Marine weapons inventory. I planned on keeping my .44 Auto Mags as my handguns. A police officer who was a friend of the family told us you needed at least a .41-caliber handgun if you wanted to be sure you were going to put a perp down. Even if you don't kill him, if you hit any part of his body, the trauma caused by that size of round will keep anyone from returning fire. Caleb and I took our .44 Auto Mags to Afghanistan and proved for ourselves our police officer friend had been correct.

Not that the Marine weapons inventory isn't extensive. There are sixteen categories of weapons from non-lethal to aircraft weapons and everything in between. Each category has several weapons to choose from. Take handguns for example. There are a total of six handguns to choose from: a couple of Berettas, a Glock 19, Colt's M45a1 CQBP (for close quarter battle pistol used by most of the Marines Recon Battalions personnel) and two SIG Sauers (M17 and M18). Both of which used 9mm rounds and were designated the standard issue of handgun for the entire Corps.

The only one I would consider as a possible replacement for my .44 Auto Mags would be the Colt M45a1 because it uses the .45 caliber ACP ammunition. however I'm just more familiar with the Auto Mag.

Many of you may not give a flying fig about the details of the weapons I selected for my new job. And that is certainly your prerogative. But for me, my choices could be the difference between life and death. If you want to skip this section, I wouldn't be offended…at least not *too* much. Let's start with the list of Marine Corps weapons categories in active use:

> Non-Lethal
> Bladed
> Handguns
> Assault and Battle Rifles
> Designated Marksman Rifles
> Sniper Rifles
> Shotguns
> Submachine Guns
> Machine Guns
> Hand Grenades
> Grenade Launchers
> Mortars
> Artillery
> Shoulder-fired Missile and Rocket Launchers
> Vehicle-Mounted Weapons
> Aircraft-Mounted Weapons

Based on what I already know about my potential Missions, I can eliminate the following:

> Designated Marksman Rifles
> Mortars
> Artillery
> Shoulder-fired Missile and Rocket Launchers
> Aircraft-Mounted Weapons

I can shoot pretty well but I'm no marksman and don't think that skill would be needed by me. Mortars, artillery and anything that requires some form of aircraft could be required for very complex missions that would require at least a squad of troops. I foresee my first three missions as solos. I think the shoulder-fired missiles and rocket launchers are just too much fire power for at least the first couple of Missions. (Spoiler alert—I received some high-level info on my first mission and I don't really need the missiles and rockets but that could change with more complex missions) As of right now, I think this is going to be pretty much a one man show, so I'm ruling them out.

Now let's see which ones I definitely need:
Non-lethal Weapons
Bladed Weapons
Handguns
Assault Rifles
Sniper Rifles
Shotguns
Submachine Guns

Here's what I think I will need from each of the above categories:

Non-lethal Weapons:
CS Gas—More commonly known as 'tear gas'
OC Spray—More commonly known as 'pepper spray'
Baton
M84 Stun Grenade

Bladed Weapons:
Ka-Bar Combat Knife

Handguns:

My own .44 Auto Mags

Assault Rifle:

MK18 Mod 1- the rifle I carried in Afghanistan

Sniper Rifle:

Barrett 50 Cal/M83A3- I was trained to use this rifle

Shotguns:

Mossberg 590A1 12-guage pump

Submachine Guns:

Heckler & Koch MP5

Next, I need to see which ones I *might* need:

Machine Guns:

Maybe M27 IAR light machine gun

Hand Grenades:

Maybe Mk 141 Mod 0 "flash bang'
Maybe AN-18 smoke grenades

Grenade Launchers:

Maybe MGL 40mm 6 shot revolver

Vehicle-mounted Weapons:

Only if I need some form of assault vehicle to accomplish my mission

The following is a more detailed description of the weapons I selected as must haves. In addition, I've included a short description of the training I went through with most of the weapons:

CHAPTER 18

Non-Lethal Weapons

CA Gas—Cry Me A River--Caleb

"The best way to learn about the effects of tear gas are to experience them for yourself," said Staff Sergeant Boone.

Joshua and three Marines fresh out of basic training at Paris Island were sitting on benches inside a small wooden building with no windows and one door. Joshua knew what was coming, he had been through this before in his first visit to Camp LeJeune. However, the powers-that-be felt he would benefit from a refresher experience. The three Marine privates (they had no rank stripes on their sleeves) had no clue what they were in for.

"In a few minutes," the staff sergeant said, "I will leave this shed and throw in a canister of CS Gas. Don't touch the canister, it will burn you severely if you do. The door will be locked from the outside and to successfully complete this test, you must remain in the room until I unlock the door. Are there any questions?"

There were none.

"One last thing. Don't worry, hardly anyone ever dies from this test but it will be uncomfortable." With that he pulled the pin from the gas canister, lobbed it onto the floor, then closed the door and locked it.

Joshua closed his eyes as tightly as he could but the three privates stared at the white gas streaming out of the dark green canister. That was a mistake. Their eyes began burning instantly causing tears to flow from their eyes in steaming rivulets. There was also coughing and choking followed by the sound of vomiting.

Joshua quickly dove to the floor and turned his head away from the sizzling canister keeping his eyes tightly closed. It made the effect of the gas almost bearable but the gas always managed to seep in anyway. He breathed through his mouth to protect the mucus membranes in his nasal passages as much as he could but he knew he would have a sore throat for a day or two.

It seemed like it lasted forever but it was really only a few minutes before the door opened and the staff sergeant wearing a gasmask herded everyone out into the fresh air. Tears were streaming down Joshua's cheeks. His throat felt raw and he couldn't keep from coughing. His nose survived pretty much intact but there was still a stinging sensation that would last for a while.

There were two lance corporals who put oxygen masks over the faces of the most affected privates. One had passed out before the door was opened and the second made it outside and began projectile vomiting, then he too lost consciousness. The remaining private seemed okay but his eyes were a bright shade of red and he continued to tear and cough.

The four test subjects were required to spend an hour before they were released. Navy corpsmen attended to the two privates who had passed out. They also handed out some type of ointment and eye drops to soothe some of the irritation.

The staff sergeant approached Joshua and said, "Well big guy, you seemed to survive intact better than the rest of them. What's your secret?"

"I've been through this before, just after I left Paris Island for Camp LeJeune, over five years ago," Joshua answered.

"Why aren't you in uniform?"

"I'm no longer on active duty?"

The staff sergeant smiled and asked, "So you came back for a rerun just for the fun of it?"

Joshua chuckled. "Hardly, I'm with another non-military government agency. It was part of my training."

"Well good luck to you, secret agent man."

When the four of them were finally released, I transported back to the BOQ, had dinner at the O-Club with Joshua and checked out what he would be doing for the next non-lethal weapons test.

OC Spray, The Eyes Have It--Joshua

After my experience with tear gas, I looked forward to my Krav Maga training the next day. By the day after, I had sufficiently recovered from the gas but now I was going to be learning about pepper spray.

This time there were six of us attending the training. Again I was the only non-marine in the group. Staff Sergeant Grimes gave us a brief overview.

"Today we are going to demonstrate the use of pepper spray. But before we get into that let me give you a brief overview. Who wants to tell me the difference between tear gas and pepper spray?"

A corporal raised her hand and said, "Tear gas is used when you want to incapacitate a room full of people and not kill them. Pepper spray is a means of subduing an individual either outside or in a confined space, again without having to kill them."

The staff sergeant replied, "Good answer, Corporal. Expanding on your answer, not only will you not kill them, you won't permanently injure them. Both of these approaches aren't lethal but they are painful for a while and allow us to subdue our enemy.

"Why wouldn't you use tear gas outside?" he asked. This time a private raised his hand. The staff sergeant nodded at him and he said, "The wind could blow the gas away from the enemy, possibly into our own troops."

"Another good answer." He turned to me and said, "Let me ask the hulking civilian about pepper spray. What part of your enemy's body would you target using pepper spray?"

"Their eyes," I replied.

"Why wouldn't the spray be blown away by the wind?"

"Pepper spray is not a mist, it's a jet of liquid, similar to water coming out of a squirt gun."

Great analogy, bro, Caleb thought to me.

"What kind of affective range would you have with pepper spray?"

"I'd think ten to fifteen feet max," I answered.

"One last question. What would be a weakness of using pepper spray?"

I paused for a moment, then answered, "There are a few weaknesses. The enemy could turn their head away from you, duck or run away before the stream hits them in the face. To be affective you need the element of surprise."

"Give this man a hand." A few clapped briefly, before the staff sergeant interrupted them. "For a civilian, you seem to know a lot about pepper spray. Are you a police officer?"

I shook my head, "No Staff Sergeant, I was a Marine in Afghanistan for two tours. I used pepper spray on many occasions."

"Thank you for your service. Why are you not in uniform?" he enquired.

"I'm on inactive duty at the present time," I answered.

"Then why are you here?"

"It's a secret."

The staff sergeant looked at me for a beat, then asked, "Would you be willing to be our first target?"

I replied with a smile, "Of course. I love getting shot in the face with pepper spray."

The corporal raised her hand and asked, "Can I shoot him first?"

Grimes nodded and said, "Sure, go for it."

We lined up ten feet apart. There was almost no wind, it would be an easy shot.

The corporal had a small, black plastic cylinder in her hand about the size of a toilet paper tube with a button on top and a small nozzle pointed towards me.

I watched as she readied herself. When she pressed down on the trigger button, a jet of pepper juice headed towards my eyes but I snapped my head to the right and the jet ended up in my ear.

The corporal screamed, "NO! That's not fair," while the rest began laughing, including Staff Sergeant Grimes.

"Sorry, it won't happen again," I said sheepishly.

We lined up again and she fired a second shot.

This time, at the last second, I bent down and pretended to tie my shoelace as the liquid fire went harmlessly over my head but she was ready for me. She ran towards me and when I looked up she shot me again, this time drenching both my eyes. INSTANT PAIN, searing heat all over my face. I went over backwards.

One of the other trainees laughed and yelled, "Shoot him again!"

Caleb shouted a warning at me, *Watch out, dude! Incoming!*

She leaped over my legs and landed on my chest, she shot me in the eyes, then shot me a third time in the mouth and nose. I thought my whole head was going to explode. I jumped up quickly, batting the black tube from her hand and knocking her to the ground in the process and grabbed a bottle of water and poured it over my face.

By then my eyes were swollen shut and I could hardly breathe. Two of the Navy corpsmen on site for just this type of emergency, grabbed me and pushed me to the ground on my back. They had some type of spray which they shot liberally all over my face, especially around my eyes. Within ten minutes I was feeling much better. I could manage to see a little as the swelling around my eyes began to dissipate.

I continued to lay on the ground and watch as the others took turns shooting each other. No one tried to avoid the shot and the shooter never fired more than once. Everyone had learned their lesson…at my expense.

By the time the session ended, I could sit up and my nose and throat had stopped burning. My vision was almost back to normal. I managed to stand up as Staff Sergeant Grimes dismissed the troops.

While the others headed out, the corporal walked over to me and said, "I'm so sorry. I got carried away. I never expected it would affect you so much."

"Don't be sorry. It's my own fault for messing with you. I admire you not giving up on the attack. You did exactly what I did to one of the Taliban I was trying to capture in Afghanistan. I missed him twice but I finally got him. Just like you did to me."

I think I embarrassed her but she smiled at me, punched me in the stomach, turned and walked away.

Baton—Caleb

The collapsible baton was one of my favorite weapons, both for defense and offense. It's small and easily concealed when collapsed and only requires a quick flick of the wrist to extend it into a two feet long fighting stick. The origins of stick fighting can be traced back to the Philippines where rattan sticks were used either in pairs or combined with a bladed weapon. In the Philippines the sticks are called escrima sticks. They are also known as kali and arnis.

The sticks, or in our case the baton, can be used as clubs to strike a variety of targets, especially joints like the elbows, wrists, knees and ankles. Of course strikes to the head are also popular. They can be used in a thrusting manner to the face and trunk targeting the liver, groin and kidneys. The sticks act as force multipliers and increase the reach of an attack. If you have never seen an escrima combat, you would be amazed at how fast the sticks move. They're just a blur and it only takes one hit to end most fights and people do die from this style of combat.

When a Marine uses a baton it is almost never against an enemy with their own baton. It is usually used as a very quick way to get an enemy to surrender by braking an arm or leg. When you practice it is normally done against a dummy (not a stupid person, more like a sturdy mannequin with sensors to measure the force of each strike).

Joshua was very good with the baton. I had seen him use it several times and I was really glad he was my loving brother. During his training sessions he broke two of the mannequins and had registered the highest strike force numbers of all the trainees. I think that's enough about that.

M84 Stun Grenade—Joshua

The stun grenade and the flash-bang grenade are essentially the same weapon. Their objectives are to temporarily immobilize the enemy. It does this with a blinding flash of light and a very loud explosion but minimal damage. It mostly causes short term blindness and deafness which leads to total confusion and disorientation. No training is required. Just pull the pin, throw it in a room full of bad guys and close the door.

Bladed Weapons

Ka-Bar Combat Knife—Caleb

This knife has been the standard for many years for most of the military. It has multiple uses from opening a letter, peeling an apple, to quietly cutting the throat of an enemy. It can be used in knife fights and Joshua spent several days of instruction working with wooden knives against opponents. But to be honest, as long as he has a bullet in one of his guns, there won't be any knife fight.

CHAPTER 19

Handguns

.44 Auto Mag—Joshua

This is my favorite hand gun. It's a semiautomatic weapon with a magazine that holds seven rounds of magnum bullets. It's been around since the late 1960s and was made famous by the *Dirty Hairy* movies. Our dad carried one as his side arm in Vietnam. During our brief leave between tours in Afghanistan, Caleb and I both bought one and we carried them with us right up to the end.

I had no idea what had happened to our weapons when Caleb was killed and I was in a comma. Shortly after the Krav Maga YouTube video went viral, I got a call from the commander of our old recon company. He was still on active duty and was now a major. He visited me in Atlanta during the Krav Maga seminar and gave me his condolences for the loss of my brother. As a parting gift, he gave me a package that contained both our .44 Auto Mags. I cried like a baby for the next couple of hours. I could tell, Caleb was just as broken up as I was. Then my brother did something totally unexpected. He gave me his weapon. I realized he would never be able to hold the weapon again, but it was the thought that counted. That started me crying again and I really had to suck it up for the last seminar.

I really haven't had much opportunity to go to any gun ranges, so I was really looking forward to getting some expert tutoring to improve my shooting skills. The night before the training started, I took both weapons out of their cases and cleaned them thoroughly with brother Caleb looking over my shoulder giving me moral support.

Once that was done, I practiced disassembling the gun in less than thirty seconds, then reassembling it, again in less than thirty seconds.

I practiced it ten times and felt pretty good about it until Caleb made me do it with my eyes closed. I was glad he drilled me on that because it was the first thing the range mentor ordered me to do when I got to the firing range. There are a variety of names for firing range instructors, range mentor is only one.

Once the range mentor, Gunnery Sergeant Daniel Craig (no relation to the actor who last played James Bond) was convinced I knew which end of the gun to point at the target, he took me to the indoor pistol range. The target I was to shoot at was on a wire and could vary in distance from seven yards to twenty-five yards. The target was a life sized silhouette of a man pointing a gun at me.

Before I was allowed to fire my weapon, the range mentor gave me some instructions on how he wanted me to stand, how I was supposed to hold the pistol, how to sight down the barrel at the target and how to squeeze the trigger. Then he had me face the target, hold my weapon without any ammunition and dry fire the gun a few times. He made a few minor corrections.

Before he allowed me to insert the magazine with live rounds into the butt of the gun he asked me, "Mr. Brown, what is the worst sin you can commit on any firing range that will get your ass kicked off the range and banned from further training faster than you can say, 'Ah Shit?'" Gunnery Sergeant Craig was in his forties, with graying hair and a colorful vocabulary. His friends called him Gunny, I was not yet his friend.

"Always point your weapon at the target, even when not loaded. Never point it anywhere else," I replied.

"That would be a big *correcto mundo.* You may load your weapon."

I picked up my pistol from the tray where the boxes of ammunition and extra magazines were placed. I made sure the barrel was pointing down range, then picked up the magazine already loaded with seven rounds, slid the magazine into the handle until it locked in place, racked the slide to chamber the first round and released the safety. Then said, "Ready to fire."

"No you're not!" shouted the gunnery sergeant. "Lay your weapon down on the tray and set your target to twenty-five yards. Then put on your sound suppressor muffs and safety glasses."

Those were rookie mistakes, bro. You need to stay focused, jibbed Caleb.

I ignored him and said, "Target set at twenty-five yards. Muffs and glasses on. Ready to fire."

"Commence firing."

I lined up the target holding the pistol in both hands as I sighted down the barrel at the center mass of the target, took a deep breath, let it out slowly and squeezed the trigger.

I did that six more times and the magazine was empty. I laid the pistol on the tray, with the barrel pointing down range.

"Cease firing!" yelled the sergeant. "Bring in your target for scoring."

I pushed a switch on the tray and the target slid up the wire until it was right in front of us.

"How long has it been since you fired your weapon at a target?" asked my instructor.

"About two years," I answered.

He shook his head and looked at me with an expression that could only be pity and said, "Son, you have a lot of work ahead of you. You completely missed the target on two of your shots and your grouping was all over the place. Let's do it again."

I went through three more magazines and there was some improvement but not much. The last time was the best, at least all seven shots hit the target.

"Okay, Mr. Brown, let's set the target to seven yards and see if that improves your score."

I did much better with the closer target but the grouping was still pretty scattered. I needed a lot of coaching and practice. When Caleb and I left for Afghanistan for our second tour, we qualified as Sharpshooters with both pistols and rifles. Just so you know, there are three levels of qualification. The lowest being marksman, then sharpshooter and the highest being expert. In my own mind, I felt I really needed to be qualified expert with the pistol before I went out on my first mission.

We returned to the BOQ and I was somewhat surprised my right hand was a little sore from the kick of the recoil. I had one day to recover physically. I was hoping Caleb would have some suggestions for improving my shooting. Little did I realize what my brother's spirit had in mind.

After I had taken a shower and gotten cleaned up, we went to an early dinner at the Officer's Club. Caleb asked if we could have the seafood pasta. That kind of caught me off guard. I usually ate whatever I wanted and Caleb would enjoy whatever I ate as if he had eaten the meal himself. If I stuffed myself and felt uncomfortable, he would share my discomfort. When I felt hungry, he would too. But he never asked me for a specific meal…until now.

Why would you want the seafood pasta, I thought to him.

When we walked by the kitchen, you could smell the aroma of it, he replied. *It smelled terrific and I wanted to 'taste' it. Unless you eat it, I can't 'taste' it.*

I don't remember smelling it.

Of course not. You were too busy feeling sorry for yourself about what a crappy shooter you are. But I'm going to fix that after dinner, if you're willing to let me help you and you order the seafood pasta dinner. What do you say?

So you're bribing me? I don't like being bribed.

Live with it, he responded.

After dinner, by the way the seafood pasta was terrific, we headed back to the BOQ and Caleb, who thanked me profusely for not eating steak, laid out what he was sure he could do to improve my shooting skills if I agreed to a few 'upgrades.'

Okay, hear me out, Josh. While you were shooting I was right with you, not manipulating anything, just observing through your eyes but also what your mind was doing, where it was focused.

I noticed three things that I think were off. The first was that your focus drifted. You weren't staying with the shot. Your mind was busy jumping around from one thought to another. You would be thinking if your stance was right or if you were breathing correctly and your vision was jumping from one part of the target to another.

So here is where I can help. First, focusing on the target. Your vision needs to be locked on to a very specific part of the target. I recommend you use one eye of the target. Second, your hand-eye coordination. Your body needs to point the gun exactly where you are looking. And lastly, you need to relax your entire body more. I know you were squeezing the trigger but at the last second you were jerking it and pulling the muzzle away from the target point. You got me so far?

I nodded. He was right but how was he going to fix me so I would overcome those problems. *So how are you going to fix me?* I asked.

With your permission, while you're sleeping, I will make some tiny adjustments that when you're shooting with any type of weapon the following will happen: Your eyes will remain focused on one spot on the target. It would work for paper targets as well as a person or a vicious animal. It could be a car tire or a person's hand. Whatever your brain chooses as the target, your eyes will lock on to it.

I'll also adjust your hand-eye coordination so that whatever your eyes are focused on your weapon will hit the target every time. It doesn't matter if it is a stationary target or a moving one. It won't matter if you're holding your weapon and sighting down the barrel or shooting from the hip. You will always hit the target.

Lastly, when you're involved in any form of fire fight, your body will not tense up. You will remain calm until the fight is completed and the threat neutralized.

That's it. What do you think?

It sounded great but to be honest, I had my doubts. I had to ask. *So Caleb, have you ever done anything like this before? I mean have you made 'tiny adjustments' to my mind and not told me about it?*

Sorry, bro. I've never made any adjustments to your mind, even when you were freaking out about me being a ghost. I helped you go to sleep on that park bench and watched over you to make sure you weren't mugged but I never tried to change your mind.

Then why are you so confident you can make all this work?

Caleb paused for a moment before answering me. The pause bothered me. I hoped he wasn't making up some cock-and-bull story to tell me. Finally he said, *I don't know how I know. I just know I can do it. I want to do it because I think it will improve your chances of surviving these missions they want you to do. Your survival is the most import thing to me.*

Good enough for me, Caleb. Do your best and we'll see how it goes the next training session. And thank you for your brilliant ideas. Together we will be an unbeatable team.

The next day I was up at 0600 hours and went through my normal routine, stretching and a five-mile run, a quick breakfast in my quarters of the food I bought at the commissary, then attended my Mandarin language class. I had a small lunch at the mess hall then had a training session for Krav Maga. Whatever Caleb did to me the night before to improve my shooting skills was undetectable. Which meant either they didn't take or he was really skilled. I really hoped it was the latter.

Dinner was at the officer's club and this time Caleb let me choose our meal, then back to the BOQ. I cleaned and field stripped both .44 Auto Mags and loaded a box full of magazines for an hour, watched a little television and went to bed at 1000 hours.

The following day, I was at the shooting range right after lunch and ready to see if Caleb had really turned me into Deadeye Dick.

"Good afternoon, Mr. Brown. Are you ready for your second session?"

"Yes, Gunnery Sergeant. I've been looking forward to doing this again," I answered as we headed out to the indoor pistol range. I had my carry-case with both .44 Auto Mags, and as many loaded magazines as I could fit in the case. My muffs and safety glasses were on top.

The instructor had me go through the dry firing drill again and he didn't make any adjustments to my stance. I had one request, "May I make one mod to the target?"

He looked at me with a quizzical expression. "What type of mod are we talking about?"

"I want to add eye balls to the silhouette," I answered.

He smiled and shook his head in disbelief. "Son, if that's what it takes to float your boat, have at it."

I took a red marker and quickly sketched two eyes, a nose and a smiley mouth. I sent the target to the twenty-five yards position, put on my muffs and safety glasses. At the gunnery sergeant's order, I loaded a magazine into one of my weapons, chambered a round, clicked off the safety and laid it on the tray with the barrel pointed down range. "Ready to fire, Gunnery Sergeant," I said.

"Commence firing," he ordered. I assumed the proper stance, brought the weapon up and sighted down the barrel. I could clearly see all of the features I had drawn on the target. I took a cleansing breath and let it out slowly and was aware I felt very relaxed.

I squeezed off seven shots in only a few seconds and placed the pistol on the tray as my instructor ordered, "Cease fire," then he added, "You got somewhere to be? You must have because you did all seven shots in less than five seconds. What's your hurry?"

I turned my head and looked back at him and said with a straight face, "I'm in the zone, Gunnery Sergeant. I'm truly in the zone."

"Horse shit," was his reply. "Let's bring in the target and see which zone you are truly in."

The target stopped in front of the tray, about six feet from us. It had seven holes tightly grouped in the head. One was in the middle of the target's forehead, one in each eye and four evenly spaced holes that went from one side of the red mouth to the other. Caleb had done it! Just like he said he would.

"Well, would you look at that? That was some shooting. You were just sandbagging me the first day you were here, right? Just trying to get ole Gunny feeling sorry for you. Telling me stories about how you hadn't done any shooting for two years. What a crock of shit that was. Okay, Mr. Smarty Pants, do you think you can do it again?"

I nodded and answered, "Sure thing. How about I do it one handed this time?"

"Now you're just bragging but I'd love to see you try."

I took a new target and marked it up with my red pen, sent it down the wire to twenty-five yards, went through all the steps again, except this time I held the gun in my right hand.

"Commence firing," came the order from the instructor and I fired seven shots almost as quickly as I did the first time.

We brought the target back to the tray and saw seven holes in the same places as the last time. The instructor's mouth dropped open in amazement. "Are we on Candid Camera or something? I don't believe your just did that. I'm being set up. Tell me the punch line."

"How would you like to see me do it with my left hand?"

"Sure thing. Why not? Fire away."

Taking Caleb's weapon out of the carry case, I loaded the magazine, marked up another target and waited.

"Commence Firing."

Same results. "Damn it, son. I must be dreaming. Nobody I know of can shoot that well."

"How about, just once more. This time with a pistol in each hand. What do you say?" I was on a role and didn't want to stop, even though Caleb had been whispering in my ear to stop showing off.

I marked up the last target and set it in position, loaded magazines in both weapons and waited.

"Commence firing!"

As quickly as I could, I fired eight rounds, alternately shooting each weapon. The result was another perfect score.

When Gunnery Sergeant Craig looked at the last target he just shook his head in total disbelief. He turned to me and said almost reverently, "Son, if you had a pussy instead of a dick, I'd be calling you Annie Oakley. You must be an android or have a computer for a brain. Nobody, and I mean absolutely nobody, has ever shot like that with a .44 Auto Mag at that distance. There might possible be some shooters with a .22 come close but I doubt it. From now on you can call me Gunny."

Gunny certified me as an expert shooter with a handgun that day. And it was all because of my spirit brother Caleb. The following week, I began the rest of the handgun training.

CHAPTER 20

Handgun Training Continued—Caleb

It's one thing to hit a stationary target, it's quite another to hit a moving one, especially when they're shooting back at you. The remainder of Joshua's handgun training consisted first of hitting moving targets and ended with live-fire activities against robot attackers.

The moving target practice reminded me of the shooting galleries at the county fair where you used a bb gun to shoot at dolls on conveyor belts. When you hit one, the doll would fall over. If you hit enough dolls you won a prize. My favorite version was the moving bear, a little less than a foot tall. When you shot it, a bell would go off and the bear would change directions. It was more difficult to shoot the bear than the dolls but the prizes were better. I won so many prizes shooting the bear, I was banned for life. That really hurt my feelings. I felt I was being punished because I was such a good shot. But enough about me and my childhood angst. Not really sure what angst is but I was told I had it.

In 2020s the Marines introduced randomly moving targets into their weapons training. Think of a man-sized R2D2-like robot that has the image of a given enemy. It consists of a four-wheel drive base with a replica of a human torso and head attached. It is completely autonomous and is manufactured by Marathon Targets. For qualifying with a pistol you're required to destroy a target coming at you from twenty-five yards. To destroy your target you have to make three kill shots, two to the chest and one to the head within five seconds.

For this training, the Marine is to be dressed in full battle gear with body armor and helmet and using his standard pistol, using live ammunition.

The training and qualification process takes a week and includes a variety of scenarios including single and multiple targets in both day and night situations. Fortunately, the robots don't carry any weapons and can't fight back. Well, sometimes they were allowed to fight back with rubber bullets.

Apparently, for Joshua's moving target training, Gunnery Sergeant Craig had designed a unique scenario with a variety of robo-targets. The mock battle field had a few battle-damaged building façades and three burned out vehicles, a car, a pickup truck and what looked like an armored personnel carrier. There was also a fountain between the wrecked vehicles and the damaged buildings.

It began with a single target dressed as a Taliban soldier, complete with turban. The face had a beard and the eyes of a fanatic. It brought back bad memories for me, probably for Joshua as well.

When the target went active, it approached Joshua from twenty-five yards at the speed of a fast run, screaming at him in Pashto, firing rubber bullets from his AK-47. The bullets pinged off of Joshua's body armor as he fired from the hip with both guns placing one shot in each eye and two in the chest.

The force of Joshua's rounds striking the target bent it backwards and it stopped immediately. A weak voice could be heard from the target's sound box speaking in Pashto. Translated it meant, "You've killed me, infidel."

I thought that was a nice touch.

Two technicians quickly ran out and moved the target onto a small flatbed trailer pulled by an ATV and took it back for refurbishment as Joshua reloaded his weapons. A few minutes later the technicians returned, this time with two new targets.

Gunny stood behind Joshua and said, "Nice shooting, Mr. Brown but I'm sure you know it's going to get more complicated." He turned and jogged behind a shield wall as the technicians placed the two new Taliban targets about twenty feet apart, twenty-five yards from Joshua. Both carried AK-47s, both looked nasty.

Through the PA system, Josh heard Gunny shout, "Commence firing!"

The two Taliban began moving quickly, juking as they moved in separate attack patterns, screaming and firing their weapons as they went.

There was limited cover but Joshua dove behind what looked like a burned-out car and briefly waited. When the first target simulated running out of ammunition, Joshua popped up and took four quick shots as rubber bullets from the second target whined all around him making pinging sounds as they bounced off the trashed vehicle.

Joshua took cover, crawled on his stomach to the other end of the car and quickly peeked around the car's trunk. The second target opened fire where he'd been a few seconds ago. Out of the line of fire, Joshua still lying on the ground, took another four shots, two to the eyes and two to the chest. There were no dying testimonials this time, just silence.

"Cease firing," came the order over the PA.

And so it went. The next round had two targets but one of the targets had a female hostage as a shield held in front. The hostage looked like a young girl and she was screaming, "Please don't kill me!"

Joshua shot the first target, the one without the hostage, and then turned quickly to the second and saw the head of the Taliban soldier over the shoulder of the young girl. He fired one shot striking the target in the middle of his forehead, snapping his head back and releasing the girl from his grasp. He now had a clean view of the target and shot him four more times.

This time the young girl yelled her gratitude, "You saved my life! You're my hero, brave American."

It sounded a little corny but it made me and my brother laugh.

There were a few more scenarios, involving first four and then five targets representing a variety of ethnic groups. There were also non-target robots thrown in to make things more complicated. This large number of targets required Joshua to reload his weapons while the scenarios were in progress. The targets used a variety of weapons to attack my brother, including flash bang grenades and even pepper spray, which I'm happy to report, Joshua was able to avoid.

During daylight, he had successfully completed six scenarios. After a short break for dinner, Josh had to return for three additional night exercises. The last one involved two robo drones who weren't specified as either targets or non-targets as well as three targets and five more non-targets. This last drill would require him to use night vision glasses for at least part of the time as all artificial lighting would be turned off. Obviously, this was the most complicated drill of all. The battle field for the last exercise was moved to a new location, a couple of hundred yards away from the original training spot.

The first two night exercises went off without a hitch. When they were completed, Gunny and Joshua climbed aboard the six passenger ATV with the technicians and headed to the last exercise site. It was a dark night, with the moon hardly visible behind the cloud cover and no artificial lighting in sight, except for the headlights of the ATV. They pulled up on the top of a knoll and stopped the ATV, the headlight shining down the hill illuminating what looked like a police patrol car.

The techs got out of the ATV and headed over the top of the hill to the protected location while Gunny briefed Joshua on the exercise. "That patrol car belongs to two border patrol officers. The car's lights are out because they are on a stakeout waiting for a coyote and his two men who are bringing a group of illegal aliens across the border into the United States. It is suspected that this coyote and his two associates have been crossing groups of illegals into the US, taking their money and killing them. Your mission is to prevent that from happening. If the coyote and his men attempt to resist, you're authorized to protect the illegals and yourself by whatever means you find necessary. Any questions?"

"What about the two border patrol officers?"

"What about them?" asked Gunny.

"Are they good guys or bad?" asked Joshua in return.

"Unknown at this time," replied Gunny. "That's all I can tell you."

The gunnery sergeant got out of the ATV and headed up the hill, "Wait for my signal to begin, he said as he crested the top and entered the protected location.

Joshua sat in the ATV and checked both of his weapons, placed them back in their holsters and waited. He didn't have to wait long. "Commence exercise. Good hunting."

He stepped out of the ATV and started down the hill toward the patrol car. When he got closer he could see two male robots dressed in Border Patrol uniforms standing behind the open front doors of the cruiser. In the lights from the ATV Joshua could see they weren't happy to see him and noticed their right hands were hidden behind the open car doors.

The older one asked, "Who are you and what are doing here?"

"I'm Special Agent Joshua Brown. I've been sent here to assist you in the arrest of the coyote and his two men and detaining the illegals."

"Who authorized you to assist us?" the younger one asked.

"Your boss asked me to assist you since this coyote is suspected of killing his illegals and stealing their money."

The two men looked at each other then began to quickly raise their gun hands. Joshua was much quicker. As their guns came in view, he shot the older one first then heard the second one curse as his gun didn't fire and he shot him before he could recover.

Immediately, he heard gun fire from down the hill and ducked down in front of the patrol car. A few more shots were made toward the ATV then it's lights were shut off. It became very dark. He put on his night vision goggles and stood up looking down the hill. He increased the magnification and zoomed in on the coyote and his two men. The illegals were nowhere to be seen. None of the coyotes were wearing NVGs and with the ATV lights out, they could no longer see him.

Joshua stood and as quietly as he could, started down the hill. When he was about thirty yards from them he said, "Do you speak English?"

"No English, *Española.*"

Joshua began speaking in Spanish, "I am a federal agent and I'm here to arrest you and your men on charges of human trafficking and possibly murder. Lay down your weapons, raise your hands and walk up the hill."

He immediately moved ten yards to his right and as he expected, the coyotes began firing at where they had heard his voice. He pulled his weapons from their holsters, turned up the magnification on his NVGs, looked into the leader's eyes and shot them both. Before his assistants could move he shot them too. It became very quiet. The only sound was from a soft breeze as it blew across the exercise site.

Joshua holstered both weapons and in Spanish, he said "My name is Joshua Brown. I am a government agent who was sent to protect you from being killed by the coyote. I will take you to safety."

There was no response, just the sound of the wind. He tried again. "This coyote has already killed other illegals like you. He promised you a better life in America, took your money and was going to kill you, just like he has killed other illegals. Please let me help you."

At first there was only the sound of the wind and Joshua wasn't sure what to do next, but then, a few moments later, he heard the voice of a young woman speaking in Spanish. "Please don't hurt us."

He raised both hands above his head and said, "Look, I have put my guns away. I will not hurt you. I promise."

Slowly, five non-targets rolled out from behind a large boulder. Three looked like women and two like men as they wheeled towards him. The first one, a young women reached him first and said to him in Spanish, "Thank you for saving our lives."

I didn't know whether to laugh or cry. Whatever I felt, I was glad this handgun portion of his training was successfully completed and he could move on to qualifying with his rifle.

CHAPTER 21

Assault Rifle:

MK18 Mod1 CQBR (Close Quarter Battle Receiver)—Joshua

This is the rifle that Caleb and I used in Afghanistan and we were both very comfortable with it. It is a modification of the Navy developed MK4, a relatively short-barreled weapon used primarily for defense. It has an effective range of a little over 300 yards and fires a 5.56X45mm NATO rounds at a rate of over 700 rounds per minute. We used the 30 round detachable magazine and it saved our butts on numerous occasions.

While it claims to have an effective range of around 300 yards most of the recon battalion troops used it for targets less than 100 yards. I believe the reason for that is that Recon Marines, like Navy Seals, Army Rangers, Delta Force and other special forces organizations take part in very surgical strikes. I consider them the spies of the military. And as such, they're involved in more close quarter battles than the rest of the military who take part in warfare on a much larger scale. That requires rifles that are accurate up to much larger distances, more like 500 yards and greater.

When the Navy Seals killed Bin Laden they used a Heckler & Koch 416 which is very similar to the MK18.

Marine infantry troops are all required to pass the Annual Rifle Qualification process. That test was recently upgraded to include moving targets mentioned in the handgun write up as well as stationary targets. The ARQ is broken into three parts. They are:

Long Bay—fire 50 rounds at stationary targets from standing, kneeling and prone positions at three different distances, 200, 300 and 500 yards.

Short Bay—fire 50 rounds at stationary targets from standing and kneeling positions at 100 yards and at moving targets at 25 to 15 yards

Night—same as Short Bay requirements.

I went through the ARQ evaluation with only a few Marines who had just been transferred into the infantry or as part of the advanced training of new recruits. I manage to qualify for expert status but only because of Caleb's upgrades. I know how to fire my assault rifle but because of the missions I was involved with, I seldom used it in a fire fight. When we left for Afghanistan I had qualified as sharpshooter but thanks to my brother, now I could never miss. Well, actually Caleb suggested I miss occasionally just so I appeared to be human but with his upgrades it was now more difficult to miss the bull's eye.

Sniper Rifle

M82A3 aka Barrett 50 Caliber

Based on what little I found out about my forthcoming missions, having a sniper rifle available could come in handy. As platoon leaders, Caleb and I had gone through sniper familiarization training, which is a lot different than what the actual snipers went through.

There were two things I remember from my familiarization training. The first is that the real snipers in our platoons preferred the M82A3. That was why I chose the Barrett over the other sniper rifles on the list. The second thing was having a spotter makes you a much better shooter. While the shooter is looking through their high-powered scope at the target, the spotter is checking on the range, the wind speed and direction, the air temperature and humidity and whether the target is above or below the shooter and by how much. All that data is fed into the computerized scope which adjusts the cross-hair position giving the shooter the best chance for a kill shot.

In my recent sniper training at Camp LeJeune, with Caleb as my spotter, I was able to make kill shots on stationary targets at a range of a 1,000 yards, which isn't too bad. It earned me a marksman badge but in truth, I never expected to have to make that shot in a mission. If I needed a sniper for a specific mission, I would request an expert rated sniper to join me to give us the best chance of a successful mission. I would also allow them to choose which sniper rifle they preferred.

Just for the record, the longest range for a successful kill shot was by a Canadian sniper. On 22 June 2017 from the top of a tall building in an Islamic State, the sniper shot and killed an ISIS fighter at a range of 3,871 yards, more than two miles. It took the bullet almost ten seconds to reach the target. The motto of snipers is, 'One shot, one kill.'

Shotgun

Mossberg 590A1 12-gauge pump—Caleb

I have to admit; Joshua and I really like shotguns. When you grow up in small towns in the deep south, everyone learns how to shoot and hunt when they're young. The first real weapons we ever owned were shotguns and our papa taught us how to shoot them. Before that, we both had Red Ryder BB guns and did a lot of target shooting. A little later, we would try our shooting skill at squirrels and rabbits. The BB guns weren't really strong enough to do any real damage but apparently it annoyed them something fierce. I based that comment on the time we shot at some squirrels who actually attacked us. Later my mama told us there might have been a mama squirrel who had a bunch of babies. She was just trying to protect her little ones.

When we got our shotguns before we ever pulled a trigger or fired a shot, our papa made sure we knew all the safety rules, he showed us how to shoot tin cans off of fence posts and boulders. When he thought we knew what we were doing, he took us out bird hunting when we were twelve.

It took us several shots before we got our first birds. Papa showed us how we had to lead the target if we wanted to hit it. "Shoot it where it will be, not where it was when you pulled the trigger. When we shot our first birds, we felt like we were big game hunters. Mama took our birds and made pigeon pie out of them. As we got older, papa bought us used 30-30 lever action Winchesters for hunting bigger game.

But we never lost our love of hunting birds with our papa and we still have those old guns somewhere in storage. Even though we graduated to bigger, more powerful shotguns, the first ones were the ones we kept.

The last time we went bird hunting with our papa was just before we joined the Marines. At that time we both had the Mossberg 12-gauge pump action shotguns. When Joshua saw them listed on Marine Shotgun List, it was a no-brainer. We both chose the Mossberg pump action over the more sophisticated semiautomatic weapons. We even had occasion to use them in combat in Afghanistan.

I believe the shotgun is excellent in close quarter situations. It's possible to take out several targets with one shot due to the way the pellets from the shotgun shells spread out when fired. Or if one prefers to use shells with a lead slug, they leave a very large hole in a specific target. Lastly, shotguns are very loud because each shell has more gun powdered then rifle ammunition. Some believe the noise is similar to that from a flash bang grenade. High noise levels usually reduce hearing of anyone in close proximity to a shotgun blast for several minutes and can even result in ruptured ear drums.

It was still a no-brainer that he chose the same shotgun for his new missions.

Training was limited. It was definitely a point and shoot weapon.

Submachine Guns:

Heckler & Koch MP5K—Joshua

This weapon is ideal for close quarter battles that I assume will be an important part of my missions. The MP5K has been around for a very long time. The German gun manufacturer introduced the MK5 in the mid-1960s and it is still part of the Marine weapons inventory. It has a number of very desirable features that I believe will be to our advantage in close quarter combat situations. To highlight a few, it is a very small weapon, the overall length a little less than 13 inches which makes it very maneuverable in close quarter situations. It has a switch that permits the shooter to select from four trigger settings: single shot, fully automatic, two round bursts or three round bursts and lastly it can fire at the rate of 900 rounds per minute. The magazine can hold 30 rounds of 9mm ammunition.

These weapons were very popular with the Marine recon troops. They're light weight, compact and easy to operate. If needed, they can saturate a room with bullets in just a few seconds. They can empty a 30-round magazine in only 2 seconds.

There are a few limitations to the MP5K, the main one being the short barrel (4.5 inches) which can reduce accuracy but when you put out so much lead so fast, you really don't have to aim.

CHAPTER 22

Planning, Planning & More Planning—Caleb

During my last tour in Afghanistan, I was involved in planning for our recon battalion. My goal here is to give you an overview of the type of planning that Joshua was briefed on in his training on planning.

There are four levels of planning that are used by businesses, governments and military operations. Those levels are:

Strategic Planning
Tactical Planning
Mission Planning
Logistic Planning

Strategic Planning establishes the long-term goals of what an organization wants to achieve. There is usually an overall goal and sub goals to be accomplished for various time periods. For example, in battle planning the overall goal could be to defeat an enemy and acquire its lands, people and resources within five years. Sub goals could include the taking of the capital city within the first year. The next sub goal could be to conquer all resistance within a twenty-mile radius from the capital city. The last sub goal would be to completely take over the entire country, put in place a new government and gain acceptance of the inhabitants of the overthrown country.

A business example could be to move into a new market area and within three years acquire a 75% share of the sales of the business's products.

A government strategic plan could be to establish a majority vote in the senate by the next election.

Tactical Planning deals with how the goals of the strategic plan can be accomplished. What would be the most effective method to reach those goals? Let's look at the strategic plan for the military example and focus on the first sub goal of taking the capitol. There could be several options. They could threaten to destroy the city by bombing if the current residents refused to surrender. They could assassinate the current leadership and install their own leaders. If they had a superior force they could do what the Nazis did with the Blitzkriegs by the rapid deployment of troops to capture the capitol before they could defend themselves. Those are just a few of the options they could select from. The planners have to decide which is the best option.

The business example also has various options on how to take over the market shares, such as introducing old products in new packaging or dropping the price of their products below the competition until they drive them out of business. Then increase the price once they dominate that market. Another approach would be to introduce new, more desirable products, such as the introduction of all-electric vehicles into a market dominated by gasoline powered models when gasoline prices are soaring.

Mission Planning could be considered a sub set of tactical planning. It takes it down to even more detailed activities. Continuing with the military example, this would be for platoon or squad level actions to take a very specific objective. A squad clearing a specific building where enemy leaders were hiding out, would be one example.

Logistic Planning involves making sure people and resources required to complete the mission objectives are made available at the proper location and time. All the planning in the world would be a waste of time if you can't get the necessary troops, weapons and supplies at the right spot, at the right time. You don't want a box of rubber duckies when you need grenades.

One last item of interest regarding planning in general. If you don't want your planning to be in vain, you have to know what your opposition is doing. In the book 'The Art of War' by Sun Tzu, a fifth century BC Chinese war lord, he emphasized the importance of learning as much as you can about your enemy before you start your planning. He recommended the best way to get that information was by using spies. He considered them invaluable to winning a war and it is reported he never lost a battle.

CHAPTER 23

Getting to Know You, Getting to Learn All About You—Joshua

Learning about planning wasn't done at Camp LeJeune. It was done in Washington DC. Once I'd wrapped up my other training, I was informed I needed to pack up my gear and get ready to travel. They gave me enough time to say good-bye to many of my instructors. Unfortunately, Gad Dagan wasn't one of them. He had another training commitment but he texted me his well wishes. Gunny gave me a framed picture of me holding the hand on the illegal Mexican girl robot as we moved up the hill with the eyeless coyote robots in the background. There was some writing on the picture in a girls handwriting, "Thank you for saving my life. You're my hero." I thanked Gunny for the memento.

A Marine chopper took me from Camp LeJeune to what used to be called Andrew Air Force Base. In 2009 the name was changed to Joint Base Andrews Naval Air Facility Washington. Boy, that's a mouthful, even longer than the full name for Washington National Airport. Good luck putting it on a T-shirt.

A limousine pulled up to the helicopter before the rotor stopped spinning. I assumed it was for me and grabbed my duffle and headed for my ride, keeping my head down, to avoid the spinning rotor.

A driver in a black livery uniform greeted me and put my duffle into the trunk and opened the rear passenger door. As I got in, Caleb thought to me, *We must be somebody very important to be treated like da rich folk,* in his best southern drawl.

Dat be us, brother, I replied in my own deep south accent.

I slid into the limo's back seat and marveled at the rich Corinthian leather. The Apostle was sitting next to me and asked, "How was your trip?"

"Short but luxurious, just like this ride. Are you going to put me up at Washington's version of the Taj Mahal. I mean, just so we keep up appearances," I answered.

He gave me a droll smile and said, "Your hotel is rated five stars but hardly compares to the Taj Mahal. We won't be spending too much time there. During the next five days, we'll be bouncing around to the alphabet agencies in and around the capital city. By the way, congratulations on the completion of your training. All of your instructors rated your performance exceptionally high. Just so you know, I didn't expect anything less from you. I understand even one of the female robo targets had a crush on you. I'd love to see her picture."

I ignored his comment but Caleb injected, *The Apostle is full of zingers today but tastefully done.*

I changed the subject and asked the Apostle, "What's on the agenda for today?"

"We get you checked into the hotel, have lunch, a working lunch in our suite, and then go by the FBI Headquarters Building to meet briefly with your point of contact at that agency."

"Wait a minute," I interrupted. "I thought you were my only point of contact. Why the change?"

"No change. I have been and will remain your primary point of contact representing all of the government agencies and any other organizations you might need for support. Having said that, if something unforeseen happens to me and you cannot reach me, there will be a limited number of secondary contacts for you to get in touch with. I'll go over this in more detail at our lunch. Our suite is secure and is swept frequently for any and all surveillance devices that could have been planted."

I interrupted again, "I haven't been assigned a mission yet. Do you really think someone could be spying on me already?"

"Absolutely! Look, I agree that it is highly unlikely any one of the bad guys you will be dealing with during your missions know you even exist, let alone where you might be. That will come later. I'm more concerned our own agencies will be trying to spy on you. They can't help themselves. It's in their blood to be paranoid. They want to be the only ones to know all the secrets. Remember, knowledge is power and our own agencies are all competing to have the most power. Therefore, the need for more knowledge which means everyone will be trying to find out more about you. For this week you're no longer Joshua Brown. Every day you will get a new name and new bona fides. Every day you will move to a new hotel. You will not eat at the same restaurant twice, no matter how much you may have enjoyed the cuisine."

Damn! thought Caleb. *I thought being a spy was gonna be fun.*

I ignored him, as the Apostle continued, "Every day you will wear different clothes, different sunglasses, speak with a different accent or pretend not to speak English. I understand you're now fluent in a variety of languages, use them. Walk with a limp one day, the next, no limp but stooped over like you have a bad back. Good spies are also good actors."

"But I'm not going to be a spy," I said with a Russian accent. "I'm a mission commander, responsible for capturing the bad guys or killing them if they resist."

"You're both," he answered in an even better French accent. "Unlike James Bond, you don't want to be noticed, however when your six foot seven and weigh 300 pounds you can't help being noticed, so try and look smaller, stay in the background if you can.

"Let me simplify this as much as I can. When you're gathering information important to your mission, you're a spy. It's better if you don't ask questions. Just listen and stay alert at what's going on around you. When you're in mission commander mode, everyone should know you're in command, you need to make a presence and act like a leader. Use a strong voice, the voice of command, an 'I don't tolerate any backtalk' voice."

Our limo slowed and pulled into a drop off zone in front of the hotel. "This is our hotel. We'll continue this conversation during lunch," he said as he got out of the limo and headed for the hotel entrance. I followed him, trying to look small and limped a little.

Once I'd finished registering as Bruce Jackson, using my new AmEx credit card, I looked around for the Apostle but he was nowhere to be seen. A Hispanic looking bellhop took my duffle and guided me to the bank of elevators. As he held the door open for me I said, *"Muchas gracias."*

He stepped into the elevator car and replied, *"De nada, señor."* and pushed the button to the 21st floor. He looked at me and smiled, and said in Spanish, "Where are you from?"

"I grew up in Puerto Rico," I replied in Spanish. "How about you?"

"El Salvador. I've been in America for ten years," he answered.

The elevator slowed, then stopped and the doors opened. I handed him a twenty-dollar bill as a tip and said continuing in Spanish, "I'll take it from here, my friend," and took the key card and my duffle from him and headed to my suite.

As I started down the hall to my room he said, "Thank you my friend. If you need anything, anything at all, just ask for Carlos."

Without stopping or turning, I waved over my shoulder and kept walking until I arrived at the double French doors to my suite. One of the doors was partially opened. I put down my duffle, reached under my coat and pulled one of my guns from the shoulder holster. Keeping the pistol partially hidden behind my body, I nudged open the door with my foot.

The Apostle was sitting on the couch reading a message on his iPad and looked up as I came into the room. "What kept you so long?"

"Spanish lesson," I answered.

CHAPTER 24

A Suite Lunch—Caleb

While my brother and the Apostle lunched on china plates with crystal glasses for their drinks, I decided to check out the suite while they ate. I appreciate fine dining but sometimes I miss chewing my own food. As Joshua took a bite of his prime rib, I could sense the flavor and aroma of the food, even the texture of the meat as he ate it and swallowed. I have to admit I miss eating for myself.

I moved from room to room throughout the suite doing my own sweep for surveillance devices. I scanned every nook and cranny in every room of the suite and found nothing, which in this case was reassuring. I had just about finished and returned to the dining area when I heard something unusual. It felt like some type of very feint electronic signal. As I moved closer to the floor-to-ceiling windows, the signal became stronger, not by a lot but definitely stronger.

The thick blackout drapes had been pulled back but the thin shears underneath offered some privacy while the sunlight could still shine through. I moved back and forth across the windows searching for the strongest signal and found it. I moved past the shears and detected a small, really tiny, almost transparent speck on the outside of the window.

They had just finished the main course of their lunch and opted for a small desserts. The Apostle selected something that looked like applesauce while Josh chose a banana cream parfait, knowing banana cream pie was my favorite. I have to admit, for a moment I forgot all about the speck on the window and savored Joshua's bite of the parfait. If I had a mouth I would have been drooling. He finished it in three bites and the sense of flavor slowly drifted from me. Back to work.

Joshua, I think someone planted a listening device on the outside of one of the picture windows. Walk with me like you want to look at the Washington skyline.

He stood, stretched and began to walk around the room, then headed to the windows and pushed back the shears. It took him a few minutes before he could see it but when he did he called the Apostle. "I think I found a bug on the outside of the window."

"Did you now? It's about time. How did you detect it?" he asked.

"I keep a scanner in my pocket at all times, especially when I come into a new room," Joshua answered. "I thought since you arrived first you would have scanned the room and I didn't need to repeat what you had done."

"What lesson did you learn?" the Apostle asked.

"I learned you're a sneaky bastard and I shouldn't trust you," my brother replied.

"How droll, try again."

Joshua composed himself, then said, "I should have asked you if you had swept the rooms but you could have said yes and I would have assumed the room was clear. I guess I should have asked if you planted any bugs, which means I shouldn't trust you."

"It was a test," the Apostle said sternly. "One that you passed belatedly. Don't make more of it than that. Now that we have finished our meal, let's get to work."

After the room service staff had cleared the remains of lunch from the table and left the room, the Apostle briefed us on who we would be visiting.

"During the next five days you're going to meet five backup contacts. None of them know the other four or even know there are other backup contacts than themselves. If you cannot reach me and you absolutely need assistance, you will call them only on your encrypted phone.

"Once we have visited each of the five, their information will be stored on your phone. They will be stored in priority order. The first one on the list will be the first one to be called. If they don't answer, wait five minutes and call again. If they still don't answer, call the second person on the list, and so on. When someone answers, you will not reveal their name or your own. Each of them will have their own code name and so will you. Any questions so far?"

"Yes," answered Joshua. "What if I follow your protocol and none of them answer. What do I do next?"

"If no one answers, you're on your own and must find other alternatives on how to successfully complete the mission. However, our analysts estimate there is a 97.3 percent probability either I or one of the five backup contacts will answer. Any other questions?"

I jumped in and thought to Joshua, *Ask him if you can choose your own code names. If you choose your own code name, you are less likely to forget it.*

He ignored me and I figured out the people in charge of code names probably already had the names picked out.

"No more questions," replied Joshua.

"Then let's head out."

From what the Apostle had said about the FBI building being within walking distance from the hotel, I assumed we would be walking. However, we went to the hotel's parking garage and got into a Tesla Model 3.

Joshua asked the question I had been thinking about. "Why are we taking a car to the FBI headquarters?"

"We aren't going to the FBI building. That's the last place we want to go. I want you to see this contact so that if you need to identify him you will recognize him. I want you to recognize how he looks, what his voice sounds like, those kind of things. Just follow my lead when we get to the meeting place."

This James Bond stuff is getting way too complicated.

Nice to Meet You Mr. ????—Joshua

The Apostle drove slowly down a crowded side street that had a Starbucks on the corner. There wasn't a parking spot anywhere on either side of the street but he slowed the Tesla to a stop beside a parked pickup truck. When he honked the Tesla's horn once, a man in a Diamondbacks cap turned and looked at the Tesla. He waved, started the truck and pulled out of the parking spot and the Apostle quickly pulled into the empty space.

I turned and looked at the Apostle and asked, "How much did you have to pay him to save that parking spot for you?"

"I didn't have to pay him anything," answered the Apostle. "He's one of the PSS, short for Parking Spot Savers. They're paid by the government to make sure government officials get a parking spot for important meetings and such."

"How early did that guy have to get here to make sure you had a place to park?"

"No idea. It probably depends on street parking trends versus time of day. I estimate it could have been an hour or two. They get paid by the minute once they park their vehicle."

"How did he know you had the spot reserved?"

"This is getting tedious, Joshua. Get out of the car so we can meet the backup contact."

We walked the half block to Starbucks. It was jammed, not an empty seat in the place. But then, surprise, surprise, surprise! The Apostle put his hand on the shoulder of a man sitting at a table for four and immediately all four men stood up without so much as a glance at the Apostle. They took their drinks with them as they walked out of the coffee house. We sat down immediately on two adjacent seats. As soon we sat down, a woman with a latte walked over and sat down in one of the two remaining chairs.

She was middle aged and looked very professional. She wore a dark gray pant suit with black heels. She had a minimal amount of facial make up and her long dark hair was tied back in a pony tail. Her face looked like if she smiled it would fracture into a million pieces.

She didn't look at us, her head was turned towards the window when she said in a deep throaty voice, "Cheetah."

It was all I could do to keep from laughing. This was the woman who was going to fill in for the Apostle? I'm doomed if I ever have to call on her.

The Apostle said in a low voice, "I'm sorry, Miss. These seats are taken."

Without looking at us, Cheetah stood up and walked away.

One empty seat was quickly filled when a man in his late thirties sat down with an iced mocha. He looked at me studying my face, then said one word, "Quicksand."

Before I could respond, the Apostle responded, "Whirlwind."

A barista brought us two espressos which we sipped without saying another word. When Quicksand had finished his drink he stood and looked at me waiting to hear my code name. The Apostle leaned over and whispered into my ear, "Tell him Cheetah."

Caleb broke into hysterical laughter that only I could hear.

Whirlwind left and we waited until our espressos were gone, then we left in the Tesla.

I wasn't sure if I could keep my sanity for four more sessions, especially when my brother kept calling me Cheetah.

And so it went for the next four days. Every morning we would leave one hotel, go to the hotel parking garage, pick up another make of car with a different color, drive to another hotel and go directly to our room. Apparently, the Apostle checked us into a different hotel the evening before the next meeting. Some mornings we'd have a room service breakfast, on other days maybe order breakfast from a restaurant and have it delivered to our new room. We never used the same delivery service, one day it would be Uber, the next Lift or maybe Door Dash.

I would go to the hotel spa and do a workout for between 30 minutes to an hour. I would never repeat the workout routine or the time of day I went to the spa. Sometime during the day, in our hotel room, the Apostle would brief me on the backup contact's agency and how he expected them to support our various missions. This would never take place at the same time. It could vary by as much as several hours. However, as soon as the briefing was completed, we went to briefly meet the agency contact.

We never met at the same location and the routine was always different. For example, one cloudy day we walked out of the hotel and the Apostle began showing me how to make sure I wasn't being tailed and if I was, how to slip the tail. The Apostle referred to it as an SDR, for Surveillance Detection Route. We walked for about an hour and I was really into it, hanging on the Apostle's every suggestion.

We came up to an intersection with traffic lights. We began to cross the street in the cross walk just as the walk/wait light changed to 'wait.' The Apostle placed his hand on my back and gave me a gentle push, saying, "Hurry to the other side, we need to lose someone tailing us."

I wasn't sure if he was messing with me but I took off on a dead run and made it to the other side of the street just as the lights changed. Waiting for me was a police officer who held up his hand. "Stop right there, sir. Do you know why I'm stopping you?"

I did a quick check over my shoulder to see if the Apostle followed me but he was nowhere in sight. I turned back and said to the officer, "Jay walking?"

The officer took off his cap and put it under his arm, took out a ticket book and began to write. When there was a substantial gap in the pedestrian traffic, the officer looked up and said, "Gobi Desert."

I was confused, then it dawned on me and I said, "Cheetah."

He ripped off the ticket and handed it to me. Put his cap back on his head, then gave me a slight smile, touched the brim of his hat and said, "Have a nice day, sir."

He turned and walked away as I glanced at the ticket. It said CIA. As I looked at it, the letters began to fade. Ten seconds later, the ticket was blank.

A car I didn't recognize pulled up next to me with the passenger side window rolled down. The Apostle was driving and shouted, "Get in before the light changes."

I climbed in, put on my seat belt and just stared out the windshield without saying a word. Then I heard Caleb's voice in my head, *Well, I never saw that coming. Did you?*

I didn't reply. I just sat their fuming, feeling like a complete idiot.

The ride back to the hotel was a quiet one, neither of us spoke. The more I thought about the last few days, the angrier I became. What was the Apostle trying to accomplish? He must have known I was upset.

When we got back to our suite, I couldn't contain my anger any longer. The Apostle took out his scanner and began sweeping the room for any bugs that might have been planted while we were out. I took out my own scanner and followed right behind him, not trusting him to do a real scan. When we finished, I couldn't contain my anger any longer.

"What in the hell were we doing out there? Was it your goal to make me look like a fool?" I wasn't screaming but I was on the verge of walking away from this 'war on crime' and never look back.

I felt that Caleb was also upset with him. *That's it, bro. He can't do that to you. Let him have it!*

His response wasn't what I expected. "Please sit down, Joshua. I will explain my actions for the last few days."

I hesitated but after a few moments of indecision, I sat down in a chair across from him. In as calm a voice I could manage, I said, "I can't wait to hear what you have to say." I may have added a touch of sarcasm.

He ignored my slightly sarcastic comment and asked me a question, "Are you a fan of Clint Eastwood, especially his early *Dirty Harry* movies?"

"Why are you changing the subject?" I asked as I could feel my frustration with this man building. "What difference does it make if I like *Dirty Harry* movies?"

I'm sure he could tell I was getting very pissed off but he didn't return the anger, "Please answer my question, Joshua," he said in an even, almost emotionless, voice.

"Yes!" I blurted out. "I like the *Dirty Harry* movies. Caleb and I watched all of them when they first came out at the movie theatres and continue to watch them occasionally on television reruns. There, I answered your question. Happy now?"

He continued to ignore my anger and asked another question, "Are you familiar with the line, 'A man's gotta know his limitations' from the 1973 movie *Magnum Force*?"

I sat there and said nothing for a few minutes trying to figure out what he meant by quoting the movie line, then it dawned on me what he was doing. Apparently, Caleb figured it out at the same time. *I think he's trying say you aren't cut out to be the black James Bond,* Caleb thought to me.

I kept starring at the Apostle, trying to figure out what to say, but I had a sinking feeling in the pit of my stomach. "So are you firing me before I even get started?"

"Absolutely not, Joshua. I'm more convinced than ever you're the perfect man for the job. Your abilities have surpassed every requirement we consider important…except one." The Apostle paused for a moment to let that sink into my thick skull. "Your spy craft skills need more work. The only way I was able to determine that was to expose you to what we just finished up this afternoon."

I felt like a huge weight was lifted off my shoulders. I leaned back in my chair and tried to relax as the Apostle continued, "Spy craft skills was only one of many requirements that we felt your position would require. But you should know, it was judged to be the least important of them all.

"None of the people we saw this week were really backup contacts. They were chosen from a pool of people we use for this type of test from time to time. The real backups will be loaded into your secure mission phone with code names and pictures. Your code name will not be Cheetah, just in case you were wondering."

Caleb interjected, *Ask him what your code name will be.*

Before I could ask, he said, "Your new code name will be Black Bond."

Caleb 'shouted' into my brain, *What a really cool name! Can you dig it?*

I said nothing but stared intently at the Apostle's face. After what seemed like an eternity (probably only a few seconds) he started to smile. "I was just messing with you. Your actual code name changes every few hours as does my code and the codes of the backup contacts. When you use your secure mission phone, the display will show your current code and the code of whom you are calling."

As he was telling me this, I could 'hear' Caleb. *Ah shit! He tricked us again.*

"I want you to know that everything I exposed you to were real things that a spy would know. Some of the things you see in spy movies are real but not to the degree they are depicted in the James Bond films. If you wanted to know what real spies go through watch *The Spy Who Came in From the Cold.* It was based on a novel written by John le Carré. The book was published in 1963 and the film of the same name was released in 1965 with Richard Burton in the lead role as a British spy stationed in Berlin during the cold war.

"Both the book and the film received many awards and both were critically acclaimed for what was considered the most accurate portrayal of what it takes to be a spy. It bares almost no similarity to the Bond movies which were exciting entertainment with very little reality.

"You will undergo additional training on spy craft related to your missions but the initial mission will require very little in the way of spying. In fact you were already introduced to it during your last handgun moving target exercise. You're one week away from shipping out to your first mission assignment. I will be briefing you on all the details starting tomorrow. Get a good night's rest. I'll see you in the morning."

"Excuse me," I said. "Since the backup contacts are real, could you tell me which agencies they come from?"

Without hesitation, he replied, "No. I'm not permitted to tell you who they work for."

I tried a different tact. "Could you tell me the name of the five agencies without matching them to the backup contact names?"

The Apostle looked like he was considering my question before he said, "Actually, there are six. In addition to Homeland Security, the FBI, CIA, NSA and the US Marshalls, the last one is based at Camp LeJeune."

"The two star?" I asked without thinking.

"What two star would that be? What are you talking about? I've already forgotten what I was talking about, maybe it never happened. Good night Black Bond."

CHAPTER 25

The Mission Always Comes First—Caleb

When Joshua turned in for the night, I checked the entire suite just for something to do. There were no bugs in the place and I made sure the Apostle had also gone to sleep. The suite was secure and I decided to take a short trip to Alexandria and the Garden of Stone, better known as the Arlington National Cemetery.

Instead of transporting directly to the cemetery, I decided to travel at a leisurely pace as if I were in a hovercraft, floating along above the traffic. It was a pleasant summer night in our nation's capital, no rain in sight, just a gentle breeze ruffling the leaves on the tree lined streets. I turned down the sound of the traffic and coasted along above the roads, raising up to glide above overpasses and dropping back down so I could watch the people walking along on such a wonderful evening.

I headed for the Washington Monument and then drifted down the entire length of the Lincoln Memorial Reflection Pool. I stopped at his monument for several moments, just to study President Lincoln's image. My emotions were beginning to build in me. If I had eyes, tears would be running down my cheeks, if I had cheeks.

I glided upward and over the Lincoln Memorial and continued west toward the Potomac River. I headed across the river via the Arlington Memorial Bridge but paused in the middle and did a 360 sweep of the area. The boats on the river with their running lights aglow reminded me of the fireflies gathered under the trees that grew along the banks of the stream which ran close to our little house. I remembered the first time I saw it when Joshua and I were very young. We both thought it was the most beautiful thing we had ever seen. More spiritual tears were flowing now as I turned west and continued across the bridge and into the cemetery.

My first stop was at the grave site for President John F. Kennedy and I noticed the eternal flame shining brightly in the night. I whispered a prayer for all the Kennedys who came after him. I rose in the air and moved across row after row of headstones, heading for the Tomb of the Unknown Soldier.

When I arrived, there was an army soldier Walking the Mat, on a square plot of ground surrounding the burial site. These honor guards were called sentinels and they wore special army dress uniforms. They were all volunteers and considered the elite of the elite. One of them was always on guard at the tomb. The site was guarded 24 hours a day, every day of the year in all types of weather. I arrived in time to see the changing of the guard ceremony. The male soldier was relieved by a female sentinel similarly dressed. I found it very moving. A plaque near the tomb spoke of the four bodies who were buried there. One was from World War I, one from World War II, one from the Korean War and the last one from the Vietnam War, our father's war.

I was drawn to our parent's grave sites. When our father passed away he was buried here in Arlington. When our mother passed, she joined him. We were able to get leave to attend the services for them. Until today, those were the only times Joshua and I had visited Arlington.

When we arrived for our father's burial ceremony, our mother had joined us. All of us were overwhelmed at the number of grave sites. There were nearly 400,000 brilliant white grave markers made from marble from quarries in Vermont and Georgia. Each weighed 250 pounds. The grave sites were laid out in rows and columns with precise spacing which gives them the illusion of a stone garden. It was a gut-wrenching ceremony for our father but even more difficult for our mother's. It was time to visit my own grave site.

I chose not to make this visit with Joshua. He had a lot on his plate and I wanted him to focus on the upcoming mission. He needed to be at his best. I would join him of course but I think I handle emotional situations better than he does. We can visit together another time.

I found my own grave marker quite easily. Visiting hours at the grave sites were from 0800 hours until 1700 hours. It was already nearly midnight when I arrived at my own grave and there wasn't anyone around including the staff who maintained the cemetery. Of course, the sentinel at the Tomb of the Unknown Soldier continued to Walk the Mat but from my grave site that tomb couldn't be seen.

I hovered close to the marker just to see if they got the inscription correct. It read:

Master Sergeant Caleb Brown
US Marine Corps
2nd Reconnaissance Battalion
2nd Marine Division

Born 1996 Died 2019
Christian
†

Everything looked okay to me. As I hovered there, I wondered what was in my casket. Did they collect all my body parts and dump them into the casket? Maybe they just cremated my remains and put the urn in the casket. Or maybe the casket was empty. For some macabre reason I felt the need to find out. I began to descend, my spirit beginning to slip beneath the grass in front of the headstone when I heard a shout. It was very clear.

Caleb, stop that! What's wrong with you?

I froze and did a quick scan of the area and saw nobody. I tried broadcasting my voice to anyone who might be hiding behind a nearby tree or perhaps a grave stone. *Hello…Is anyone there? Hello? Who's calling me?*

"Oh, for crying out loud it's me, your spirit guide. Now stop all this non-sense."

All of a sudden, I was no longer in Arlington National Cemetery. Instead, I was back in my wonderland set with all the pretty trimmings. I also had a make believe body to go with my make believe wonderland. And here came my spirit guide and he didn't look happy. "Are you trying to get yourself unbonded? If you are, keep it up. You can visit your grave site but you're not allowed to go digging around in your remains. Do you understand me, Sergeant?"

I said, "Yes sir!" Then came to attention and almost saluted. I mean, after all, he was my commanding officer at one time. Or at least he looked and acted like my commanding officer.

"I don't have time for this crap. Listen up, you have new orders. But first, you have received a commendation for your support of your twin brother Joshua, during his training. You also received a special acknowledgement for developing your method of rapid language learning. That was the first time anyone successfully made it happen. Congratulations on your awards."

He paused, a look of distaste replaced his congratulatory smile. "Now the bad news. I'm sorry that I have to pass on these orders to you. I argued with my…superior and was told to shut up and follow orders. Your orders are as follows: Joshua will have three successive missions, each one being more complex than the one before it. It is estimated this could take from six months to a year to complete. Until the third mission is completed, you're to have no direct contact with your brother."

If I had a jaw, it would have dropped open in disbelief. Then I realized my avatar's jaw *did* drop open. I was so shocked, I couldn't think of what to say. The only words I managed to mumble were, "That's impossible!" I took a deep breath and all of a sudden, I couldn't stop protesting. "Joshua needs me on those missions. We're bonded. Are you going to completely separate us forever? Why are you doing this?"

I was really revved up. I had about a million things to say and questions to ask but when my commander raised his hand, I could no longer speak. He looked at his watch (what the hell does a spirit need with a watch) and said, "I'm running out of time but let me wrap this up."

I yelled at him, "Didn't you tell me time had no meaning for spirits? How can you run out of time?"

"An excellent question but for another time. The main reason for restricting you is to see what Joshua can do on his own, without any assistance from you. You will still be bonded to him, you just can't communicate directly to him. On special occasions you may be allowed to drop a hint or two which he will think was his own idea. That's all I have time for. See you next time. Bye."

He was gone. Suddenly, I was hovering over my own grave. I had no idea how long I was there. I was looking for a way around my orders. I had a very strong suspicion I had no choice. I needed to inform Joshua of the situation but I wasn't sure about when I should tell him. I didn't want to tell him just before he began his first mission, nor did I want to tell him before he began the first Mission briefing. I knew he would be too distracted in either case. It would be like before we were bonded. Neither one of us would want to live through that again. There just wasn't a good time to tell him. Time! There's that damned word again.

CHAPTER 26

First Mission Planning—Joshua

The next day, after my workout was completed in the hotel's spa and followed by a room service breakfast, we began planning for the first mission.

The first thing we covered were the mission requirements. Those requirements were generated by the Apostle and high-ranking agents from organizations that would be involved in the mission.

I was kind of surprised I hadn't heard much from Caleb. He didn't give me his usual wakeup call or tell me what he did during the night while I slept. I tried to communicate with him but all I got in return were brief comments, *I'm fine, Joshua. Just listening to the mission briefing.*

That was the extent of our communications during the entire briefing, which wasn't like him at all. Something was bothering him but I had no idea what it was. I just had to wait him out. I knew he would let me know what it was in his own time.

"This is your mission statement," began the Apostle. "You will receive one of these before each of your missions. A good mission statement should supply you with all your objectives and an outline of your expected actions, like who you are sanctioned to kill or detain and under which circumstances. This mission statement is very specific. That's because it's a very simple mission. Follow-on missions will become more complex and require a great deal more preparations to insure the mission goals can be accomplished. Any questions so far?"

"None," I replied, then asked Caleb, *How 'bout you, bro?*

Nope.

The Apostle continued his lecture. "Each mission statement will be presented in the same format. First comes a general statement of the problem. That would be followed by the mission goals. It could take a single sentence or several paragraphs to present you with what is considered needed information. The next would be the location or locations where the mission will occur. Following would be the number of participants, by name if they are known, after that, a list of weapons and equipment required to accomplish the mission. Lastly, the date and time the mission is expected to begin. Understood?"

I nodded and thought to Caleb, *You good?*

Yep.

Once we were done with mission briefing, Caleb and I were going to have a long talk about what was bothering him. But until then, I wasn't going to bother asking him for his opinions on the mission.

The Apostle connected his secure, air gapped, computer to the hotel's large, 60 inch Vizio television so it would be easier to see. He hit the enter button and the screen was filled with everything the Apostle had described.

Mission Statement:

We have received several reports from various sources that a coyote has been operating in southern Arizona who is crossing illegal aliens across the Mexican/American border. It is suspected that once into Arizona, the coyote takes their money and then murders all of the illegals. It is also rumored that one or more Border Patrol officers are involved. The rumor hasn't been substantiated and the suspected patrol officer(s) haven't been identified. Another crossing is anticipated within two weeks' time from the date of this mission statement.

Mission Goals:

- Prevent the death of all the illegal aliens

- Capture the coyote and any of his assistants, if they resist, eliminate them

- Determine the involvement of any Border Patrol officers and deal with them accordingly

- Remove the illegal aliens to a safe place

Participants:

- One or more unidentified Border Patrol officers

- The coyote known as El Jefe and at least two of his assistants

- An unknown number of illegal aliens: estimated to be between 10-20 persons (men, women and children) based on previous captures

Location(s):

- Approximately 15 miles west of Nogales, Arizona. A rancher reported the discovery of what he suspected were the remains of 10 to 15 human beings. Cause of death undetermined at this time (See the coordinates of the location in the appendix to this statement)

- Nogales, Arizona. A small boarder town (pop. 20,000 est.) adjacent to the Mexican border: main access through I-19

- Nogales, Sonora, Mexico, shares the border (pop 265,000 est.)

Timing:

- El Jefe usually brings a group of illegals into Arizona about every two weeks; he was seen in Nogales, Arizona, six days from the date of this Mission Statement

Required Weapons and Equipment:

- Handguns
- Pepper spray

- Baton
- Night vision glasses
- Zip tie cuffs
- Body Armor
- Large vehicle capable of seating 25 people
- Water bottles and packaged food

We read through all of the material several times and discussed how I was going to pin down the location and timing for El Jefe to make his next trip into the Arizona desert. For every question I had, the Apostle had an answer.

My first question wasn't related to the mission statement. Well, at least not directly. "I noticed my last handgun training exercise looks suspiciously like the mission plan. Care to comment on that?"

He paused for a moment, considering what he could tell me, then said, "A two star general, who will remain nameless, coordinated with a certain gunnery sergeant, also nameless, put together your last handgun training exercise. That's all I can say.

"I thought the two star wasn't read into my mission."

With a small smile, the Apostle, replied, "What two star? I cannot confirm or deny I know any two star general. Let's move on, shall we?"

I nodded and he continued.

"The Border Patrol cruisers are all wired with location transponders. I have access to their database and can watch to see when any cruiser heads out in that general direction. That would be your key to get ready to party.

"We also know the approximate location El Jefe will take the illegals based on where the dead bodies were found by the rancher. We also have informants who keep an eye on El Jefe and will let me know when he begins his next run.

"When the Border Patrol cruiser stops somewhere very close to the dead bodies we have all we need but you need to be on your way when the cruiser is halfway to the target location."

I changed topics. "Where can I get a truck or a bus to transport the illegal aliens?" I asked.

"I got that covered," he said. "I've made arrangements for you to 'borrow' a school bus. That would be your ride out to the target area and used to transport the illegals into Nogales, Arizona. All the buses for the Nogales school system are kept at one location. We will make arrangements for you to get the bus undetected. It would be a nice touch if you could return it when you've completed your mission."

"Those buses are a bright yellow, aren't they?" I asked. "Won't it seem unusual for a school bus to be driving around the city around midnight?"

He shrugged his shoulders and answered, "Maybe but highly unlikely. Nogales is a small town, not a huge city like Phoenix or San Diego. There won't be many people out late at night and those who are and see a school bus probably aren't going to report it."

I thought for a moment, then asked, "Let's suppose I have a bus load of illegals. Where am I supposed to deliver them when I bring them back to Nogales or do you have another location in mind?"

"You're to take the illegals to Sacred Heart Catholic Church in Nogales, Arizona. They have a history of giving temporary sanctuary to illegal aliens. Any other questions?"

I couldn't think of any so we wrapped it up with the understanding I could ask more questions as they occurred to me. The Apostle left the suite to take care of some of the pending logistic issues. It was time for me to confront my brother.

CHAPTER 27

What's Up, Pussycat—Caleb

I knew it was the best time for me to share the bad news with Joshua. Just by the way I was acting while he and the Apostle went over the Mission plan, he knew I was upset.

Once he was sure the Apostle had left the hotel, he bolted the door to make sure housekeeping or the Apostle didn't barge in unannounced. Then projected to me, *What's bothering you, Caleb? Why were you so quiet during the Mission briefing?*

I got some bad news last night, I replied.

Last night? Did you go cruising last night after I went to bed?

Yeah. I took a leisurely trip and ended up at Arlington National Cemetery.

I thought we were going to go together. His thoughts sounded like I'd hurt his feelings by going without him.

We will, Josh. I promise we'll go together but not until you're finished with your Missions. I just wanted to see my grave marker and maybe see what was in my coffin. I know that sounds weird but I wanted to know.

So where did the bad news come in. Were you disappointed about what you saw in your coffin? he asked.

I never got the chance to find out. My spirit guide stopped me. He's the one that gave me the bad news.

Joshua looked worried. *What did he tell you?*

Well first he gave me some good news. I received an accommodation for assisting you in your training and a special award for demonstrating how to learn a new language at a very fast rate.

You earned them, Caleb. I would have never learned all those languages so quickly if you hadn't made my brain adjustments. But what was the bad news?

I'm not allowed to communicate with you once you begin your initial Missions.

His worried look changed to an expression of total disbelief. His legs buckled and he sat down quickly into one of the easy chairs. When he finally spoke, his voice was only a whisper. *They can't do this. I need you with me. We're a team. I can't possibly do this without you.*

He looked on the verge of a nervous breakdown. He had come so far from the VA hospital. I couldn't let him regress back to that condition. In a firm 'voice,' I thought to him, *Yes you can, brother. You have to for the both of us. This isn't a permanent condition. It's only for the first three missions, then we can communicate again. It's only a test. Just one more test. I know you can do this.*

I stopped the telepathy for a few moments and did a quick scan of his vital signs. They were gradually trending toward normal, thank God for that.

Listen, Joshua. And please remember this. I will always be with you when you're involved in these missions. I'll be right by your side, no matter what happens. I just won't be able to communicate with you until the three test Missions are over. You hear me?

There were tears in his eyes as he nodded his head. *You need to get cleaned up before the Apostle comes back. It's been a long day. Why don't you take a shower and relax. We can watch a Dirty Harry movie later tonight if you want. I guarantee we will get through this. It'll be a piece of cake.*

He got up from the chair and headed towards the bathroom. He reminded me of one of the zombies in the *Curse of the Living Dead.*

When he finished his shower, I suggested he take a nap until the Apostle returned. He agreed and I gave him the slightest of suggestions to relax and sleep. Five minutes later he was fast asleep. Later that evening, he and the Apostle had room service dinner and the three of us watched *Dirty Harry,* the first of the series. Joshua slept well that night.

CHAPTER 28

Arizona Here We Come—Joshua

Early the next morning, the Apostle got a phone call. By 1000 hours we were boarding a C-17 at what used to be called Andrews Air Force Base (the current name is just too damn long) for a flight into Davis-Monthan Air Force Base located in Tucson, Arizona. A rental car was waiting for us outside the flight operations building. It took a little over an hour to drive down the I-19 freeway to Nogales and check into the Americana Hotel. The Americana wasn't exactly a five star hotel, but it would do.

This was our first time in Arizona and I have to admit it was hot. Granted, it was a dry heat but when it's over 110°F who cares. When I stepped out of our air conditioned car, it felt like I was stepping into a blast furnace. We had arrived in the late afternoon which we were told was the hottest time of day.

From a weather standpoint, southern Arizona reminded me of the deserts of Afghanistan only it was hotter in Arizona and maybe a little dryer. I had been instructed by the Apostle to drink lots of water. He had said, "You sweat a lot in the Arizona heat but the humidity is so low, less than ten percent in the summer, the sweat evaporates quickly so it's easy to get dehydrated. Always keep a couple of bottles of water with you at all times and avoid exposure to direct sunlight as much as you can."

When I walked into the hotel lobby, it was a welcome relief from the heat. I don't have any idea how people survive in this heat without air conditioning. I registered at the front desk, walked up the stairs to the second floor and down the hallway to our room. Caleb and I were in constant conversation with each other. We had been, ever since we began our trip to Arizona. It was our way of making sure the spirit world had not shut down our contact with each other. We knew it was coming soon but weren't sure of exactly when.

When we entered our room, it was really warm. It was obvious the A/C hadn't been turned on. I guess the hotel management wanted to save a few bucks on their electric bill. The first thing I did after dropping my duffle was to turn it on and crank the thermostat down to 65°F, the lowest setting possible. I stood in front of the vent to make sure it was working. When I felt the first signs of cool air, I unpacked my duffle.

It took about fifteen minutes for the room to cool down. I turned on the TV to a local news channel and the first thing I saw was the weather report. An attractive weather woman was giving the current conditions for the weather in southern Arizona and the five-day forecast. "The temperature in Tucson is currently 112°F and will remain above 100 until after midnight. This warm weather will continue for the rest of the week and into the weekend with high temperatures expected to peak at 115 degrees. The temperatures in the Rio Rico and Nogales areas may be a few degrees cooler."

I 'heard' Caleb moan, then think to me, *I never knew it could be this hot. How do the people here withstand this heat?*

They get used to it, I answered.

Do you think the people in hell get used to it? No man, this is torture. Why do they stay here?

Because their winters are like the rest of America's summers, I replied as I changed channels and found a local channel playing a rerun of the original Star Trek series with Captain Kirk in charge of the starship Enterprise. Caleb and I had grown to love this show. It was already in reruns when we first started watching it in our pre-teen years. Our papa bragged about how he watched it when it first came out. The Next Generation was even better but the original was a classic.

Caleb and I watched for a while, repeating the dialog right along with the actors. During a commercial break, my stomach began to growl at me. I had a couple of box lunches on the C-17 flight out of Washington and they were beginning to wear off.

I thought to Caleb, *I'm getting hungry, are you up for real Mexican food?*

Sounds fine to me. Can we wait until this episode's over? I don't want to miss watching Kirk kissing Uhura. It was the first time a white man kissed a black woman on TV.

I can wait but why are you telling me that? I watched this episode with you about a hundred times. I know all about The Kiss, same as you.

The commercials ended and Caleb shushed me. We watched The Kiss and the end of the episode and I asked Caleb if he was ready. When he discovered the next rerun was The Beverly Hillbillies he decided he could pass on that one and we drove to the La Cabaña, a Mexican restaurant a short drive from the Americana. We could have walked but it was still too damn hot to be walking.

I was really hungry and ordered two dinners. I wasn't into spicy food so I ordered a three shredded beef taco plate with rice and beans along with *sopa de queso* and a chicken *chimichanga.* I also ordered a cheese crisp with salsa and a bottle of Modelo beer while I waited for the main courses.

I ordered everything in Spanish just to keep in practice. My server, a woman in her early twenties seemed surprised to hear me speak her language. After she gave the cook my order she returned to our table and sat down opposite me and said in Spanish, "Your Spanish is perfect. You speak like you are from the border area of Mexico. Where are you from?"

I answered her in Spanish, "I'm from the state of Georgia, in the United States."

That made her laugh. "No really, where are you from. You speak like a native. I've never met a gringo who speaks that well."

Again in Spanish, I said, "I had excellent teachers. I'm starving. Is my food almost ready?" I asked, trying to change the subject.

She didn't answer. Instead, she leaned closer, studying my face. "Are you from Puerto Rico? I have heard there are many black men who grow up there and speak Spanish but they have a different accent."

I wasn't sure how to answer her but then the cook was ringing a bell signaling my dinner was ready. Caleb thought to me, *Saved by the bell. I thought she would never leave.*

She brought all my food on a huge metal platter just as a large party came in. While I ate, she was busy taking care of them. Once she finished with their orders, another group entered. Both Caleb and I agreed the food was outstanding. It tasted delicious and the portions were enormous. I needed a second Modelo to help wash it all down.

We were ready to leave and I waved at the young woman to get her attention. She had a beautiful smile as she came to our table with the check. I looked at the bill and noticed a message at the bottom. The bill was for twenty-five dollars and change. After reading her message, I put two twenties on top of the bill and said, *"Muchas Gracias, Senorita, por todo."*

I stood and pocketed the receipt indicating she should keep the change and headed for the door. Caleb asked, *I saw she left you a note but I didn't get the chance to read it. What did it say?*

As I walked out the door, I heard her say to the older woman who worked the counter, *"Que guapo el hombre, y rico tambien."*

Caleb asked again as the restaurant door shut behind us and I climbed into our rental and drove away. *What did the sever write on the note?*

I smiled as I thought to him, *She said her name was Carmelita and she wrote down her phone number. Underneath the phone number was a lipstick print of a kiss.*

I heard what sounded like a slight squeal of delight just before Caleb said, *Oh my God, the Black Bond really exists.*

CHAPTER 29

Recon, Nogales Style—Caleb

As Joshua drove out of the La Cabaña parking lot, he asked me how much time we had before the next Star Trek episode. I told him it would be at least two hours before the episode with the sexy girl robot and the robot copy of Captain Kirk. We agreed we needed to get back to the hotel to see "…where no man has gone before."

Next, he asked me for the address of the Sacred Heart Catholic Church. I accessed the address from my spirit database (so much better and faster than Google) and told him to head south on Grand Ave which turns into a one-way street called N. Arroyo Blvd. The church address was 272 N. Rodriguez St, one street west of Arroyo. It was only few miles from the hotel.

The church itself was an impressive structure built on the top a stone mountain about two hundred feet above Arroyo Blvd. It was built in 1910 and is one of the largest churches in the area with its entrance on the east side and two parking lots, one on the south side and one on the west.

We drove up the steep hill to the rear parking lot, parked the car and Joshua walked up to the front entrance. The main doors to the lobby were open and some type of service was being conducted. We stayed in the lobby area and I checked the walls for some type of emergency exit plan. I found one on the south lobby wall. It showed the entire floor plan of the church, including the rectory and a basement with a large cafeteria. Most importantly there was an outside door situated between the rectory and the cafeteria.

Joshua used his smart phone and took pictures of the floor plan and we left the lobby. We headed out to the parking lot and it only took Joshua a few minutes to locate the door to the basement area.

We still had an hour to find where they kept all of the school buses. We found them in a large parking lot a couple of blocks east of the Americana. The yard was surrounded by an eight feet high block wall. There were two large metal gates one on each side of the lot. I was able to float my presence over the wall the take a count of the number of buses. I counted twenty-eight buses parked side by side in two rows of fourteen located on the north side of the lot. On the south side, in the middle was a one story office building. On either side of the office were maintenance bays, some with special bus size hydraulic lifts. Sandwiched in between the bays were three diesel fuel pumps.

Both of the gates were motorized and I was sure they could be opened by remote controls in each bus and the office as well. As far as security goes, there were CCTV cameras on each of the four corners of the office building as well as four additional cameras mounted on fifteen feet high poles at each corner of the yard. I couldn't tell for sure if any of the cameras were stationary or scanning. I couldn't detect any movement after watching them for a few minutes even though a bright red light was visible from the front of each camera. I was positive I could take care of the cameras as well as opening a gate to 'borrow' one of the buses. But I was just as positive I wouldn't be permitted to help. The best I could do is brief Joshua on what I saw and how to disarm the security devices. That really sucks.

Our last stop (or maybe drive by) was the Border Patrol headquarters. Their offices were co-located with the local police in the town's government complex which was just a few blocks north of the Americana on Grand Ave. We took note of the secure parking lot adjacent to the police/border patrol offices. We also took note of the large selection of communication antennas mounted on the roof.

The BP offices on Grand Ave were for the investigators. Most of the BP officers were located about ten miles north of the town on the

I-19 check point. We had passed through the check point on our way down from Tucson.

We had just about wrapped our tour when Joshua received a call from the Apostle. He told him there was a trunk waiting for him at the hotel and that he was pretty sure El Jefe was going active tonight or tomorrow night at the latest. He said, "You need to get prepared to go live very quickly."

Damn, that meant we were going to miss the Star Trek rerun. And it was such a good episode.

We returned to our hotel and had the trunk delivered to our room. It didn't look so much like a trunk, more like a vault on wheels. The minute we tried to figure out how to open it, Joshua received a text message on his secure phone with a code that permitted us to open the trunk and access to all sorts of goodies.

Inside the trunk were all the things Joshua would need to carry out his mission. There was XXXL body armor, ten extra magazines preloaded with the magnum rounds for his .44 Auto Mags, a collapsed baton, two pepper sprays dispensers, a carton of six flash bang grenades, a XXXL sized Border Patrol uniform with matching cap and utility belt. The belt had two black leather holsters designed for his pistols. There were also a pair of size 13 black combat boots, night vision goggles, a body cam and a high voltage stun gun which wasn't on the Marine's list of nonlethal weapons but an excellent addition. At the bottom of the trunk was a case of forty water bottles and twenty MREs (That's Meals Ready to Eat for those of you who aren't familiar with the military acronyms) and a bag full of assorted snacks.

There was a large brown envelope taped to the inside of the trunk lid. Inside the envelope were two sets of car keys, or in this case, bus keys with the bus numbers attached to their respective key fobs. There was also a small drawing showing the location of the buses involved with the missions. The two buses were next to the west corner block wall. There were instructions indicating he would need to pull out the bus in the front row, then move the bus behind it out into the center of the yard. The front row bus was then to be backed into its original location, blocking the view of the empty space where the mission bus had been parked.

There were two more items in the envelope. One had a tag which said, 'Use Me First.' It was a remote switch that would shut down the eight CCTV cameras just before Joshua entered the yard. After he had exited the yard in the mission bus, he was to turn the cameras back on. The second item was a remote to open and close the gates. The goal was to accomplish the 'borrowing' of the bus in five minutes. All the necessary supplies would be loaded onto the bus once it was outside the gate.

I could sense a feeling of urgency building in my brother. He sorted the contents of the trunk into three piles, one for the water, MREs and snacks to be loaded onto the bus. He would load that into the trunk of our rental. Another pile was for the BP uniform with its utility belt and everything that would be attached to it. He would put that on in the hotel. The third pile was for the things he would put in a small backpack he would take aboard the bus for items he might use during the mission.

Once the sorting was done, Josh stuffed the third pile into the backpack and set it by the door. He then moved the water and food next to the door as well. He stepped into the hall and disappeared for a few minutes before returning with a luggage dolly. He quickly loaded the water, food and backpack onto the dolly and took it all out to our car and loaded it into the trunk. He returned and turned on the television just in time to watch the Star Trek episode as he dressed in the BP uniform.

He was ready for the mission to begin but while we waited for the Apostle's call, we were able to relax a little and enjoy the episode of Captain Kirk teaching a very sexy female robot about love. The credits were rolling on the screen when the Apostle called. The mission was on tonight.

Joshua turned off the TV and scanned all the rooms and closets to make sure he hadn't forgotten anything. He put the room key on the counter, left the A/C on artic cold, turned off the light and left, closing the door behind him. We wouldn't be coming back.

CHAPTER 30

The First Mission, Let's Dance—Joshua

We drove the few blocks to the school bus maintenance yard and parked in the darkest spot we could find, relatively close to the west gate. I took the 'Use Me First' remote and aimed it at the yard. Caleb was checking the cameras as I pushed the off switch.

All of the cameras are down.

How can you be sure? I asked.

Because all the little red lights on the cameras went dark, he replied.

I picked up the second remote in one hand and the two bus keys in the other. I left the car and ran quickly and quietly to the gate, pushed the button and watched the gate slide open. I ran to the front bus on the west side of the yard, jumped inside and started it up and drove far enough forward to get the rear bus out. I left the front bus idling and ran back to the mission bus, started it up and pulled it close to the open gate. I jumped out and ran back to the front bus and backed it up into the front row, turned off the engine and ran back to the mission bus, put it into drive and drove it out of the yard, closing the gate behind us. I parked the bus in the street next to the yard wall, across from the rental car. Then I picked up the 'Use Me First' remote and turned the security cameras back on.

Caleb had been timing me as I borrowed the mission bus. He thought to me, *Four minutes and fifty-two seconds. Great job, bro.*

I ran across the street to the rental, popped the trunk and carried the water, food and snacks into the bus. I ran back to the rental, closed the trunk and threw the car keys on the seat, locked the doors and ran back to the idling bus.

I took out my secure iPad and punched in the code the Apostle had given me. A map appeared on the screen showing my location and the location of the suspect BP cruiser. It also showed me the best route to follow the cruiser.

As I drove up to the stop sign at Grand Ave. a familiar voice said *"Hola me amor,* turn left onto Grand Ave. Your next turn will be in 2.5 miles. I miss you so much. *Dame un beso."*

It was Carmelita's voice. *Not now, Caleb,* I shouted at him. *I'm on the mission now. No time to fool around.*

As I drove up to the next turn it was Caleb's voice giving me directions and updates on the position of the BP cruiser. I was gaining on him as we headed out of town going west.

It didn't take long before we ran out of civilization. It was all desert, with cactus and palo verde trees. It was after midnight and very dark. There wasn't much traffic on the road and I was concerned the BP officers might see my headlights. Caleb made a good suggestion. *They're only a few miles away from you. Turn off your lights and follow their taillights. The road's pretty straight. You might want to put on you NVGs.*

Caleb was right. As I slipped the NVG over my head and in front of my eyes, night was turned into a bright green day. I turned out my headlights and moved the bus within a mile of the cruiser.

After a few minutes they turned off the highway and began to follow a dirt road into the desert. I dropped further back, I was concerned they might hear the noise of the bus's engine if I got too close.

After about five minute the car came to a stop and turned off its engine and head lights. I immediately stopped the bus and shut down my engine. It got very quiet all of a sudden and very dark.

Caleb thought to me, *I don't think they're on to you, Josh. You did a great job of tailing them.*

There was a pause, then I heard my brother's voice inside my head. *I have to go, Josh. Good luck on your missions. Remember, I'll always be with…*

He was gone. I was on my own now and I had this sinking feeling I wasn't going to be able to do this on my own. But then I realized, I wasn't alone. I could still sense his presence, I just couldn't communicate with him. But I knew, I could feel, he was still there. And that was enough.

I started the bus and moved down the hill towards the cruiser.

This concludes 'The Book of Caleb'
If you enjoyed this book and would like to find out how Joshua's first Missions went, turn the page and read the introduction to 'Joshua,' the first book in the Joshua series. If you find the introduction to Joshua intriguing, please purchase a copy of the book and enjoy the details of all three of his trial Missions.
If you liked the first book, you'll love second book in the series titled: "Joshua and Caleb" They're together now, working as a team in New Orleans to take out the major drug cartels in the western hemisphere. This isn't a trial Mission, it's the real thing. People will die.

JOSHUA

by

Frank G. Davis

INTRODUCTION

The Border Patrol vehicle sat on a slight rise above the desert plain with its lights off and the motor shut down. It was a hot summer night without any breeze and both officers sat quietly waiting with all the windows opened. It didn't help much; both men were sweating profusely.

The one on the passenger side was scanning the desert below with his night vision goggles. There was no moon this night and they were at least fifteen miles from Nogales, far away from the lights of the city. The driver checked his watch, then said in a quiet voice, almost a whisper. "Damn that El Jefe. He's a half hour late."

"Patience, Bull, he's a Mexican. They're never on time," his partner replied, also in a low voice. Sound traveled at night in the desert and they wanted to make sure no one could hear them.

Five minutes later, Bull's partner, Jake, whispered, "He's coming; just over that ridge, dead ahead."

"How many does he have this time?" Bull asked.

"Hard to tell at this distance, a dozen, maybe more. They're ten minutes out from the kill zone."

Bull snickered and replied, "More like the party zone."

Ten minutes later, the group stopped in a dry wash bed and waited.

"Do you have a positive ID on El Jefe?" Bull asked.

Jake could hear the excitement in Bull's whispering voice. He was a rookie and this was only his third encounter with a coyote. Jake wasn't sure he was going to work out. "Yes. I've got a positive visual and he's standing exactly on the coordinates I gave him. I count a total of fifteen illegals; ten women and five men, four of the women look like teenagers."

"I can't wait. Let's get this party started," Bull said as he quietly opened the car door and began to slide out, but Jake grabbed his arm.

"You still have your body cam on. Take it off," Jake ordered.

"Relax, partner. It's disconnected from the car recorder. I hooked it up to my personal recorder so I could replay the fun I'm about to have anytime I want." Bull pulled his arm free and left the car.

Jake got out of the car shaking his head. *This new guy wasn't going to work out,* he thought to himself. *Too much testosterone and not enough brains.*

Both officers walked quietly down the hill and were within ten feet of the group when Jake spoke up, *"Greetings Jefe. You're late,"* he said in Spanish.

The man jumped at the sound of his voice, *"Chingado, hombre. Don't ever sneak up on me like that again. You scared five years of my life away."*

"That's what you get for being so late. Did you forget your Rolex this time?" asked Jake.

"It took longer to go around the last site. I didn't want any of these new people to see the bodies of the last group or even smell the rotting flesh. It might have spooked them."

El Jefe turned to look at the men and women who had crossed the border with him and his two helpers. The illegals looked exhausted, both physically and mentally. They had not eaten and had only a little water for the last two days. Each of them had paid El Jefe three thousand dollars to come to the land of opportunity, to get a start of a new life.

Bull was inspecting them, seeing which women he wanted to party with, touching their breasts, or their butts, looking for the "prime stuff" as he called it. He'd seemed to have narrowed it down to three women. He had casually thrust his hand between the youngest one's legs and grabbed her crotch, just to see how she would react. She screamed and slapped his face. Bull slapper her back, knocking her off her feet and onto her back. He stood over her and began to remove his pants when Jake interrupted his fun.

"Bull, business first, then play. Get over here."

Reluctantly, Bull pulled up his pants and joined Jake and El Jefe."

Jake said, "So I count fifteen people at $3000 a head that makes $45,000 total. We're going to take $25,000 and you get $20,000."

El Jefe began to protest, but Jake interrupted, "I know what you're going to say. Our deal was a fifty-fifty split. But you were late and we have to get you to Nogales so you can get back to Mexico without other Border Patrol or ICE people finding you and your men. So, consider the extra $2,500 as a late fee and shipping and handling."

El Jefe was smoldering but no matter how much he argued, Jake was firm. Finally, he shrugged his shoulders and turned away. Bull quickly turned back to the 'wet backs' as he liked to call them, even if every river bed in this part of Arizona was dry as a bone. He unzipped his pants as he walked back to the young girl still lying on the ground.

That's when they heard it. It sounded like a big truck. It seemed to be coming down the same dirt path the two Border Patrol officers had taken and they raced back to their SUV, Bull zipping up his pants as he went. El Jefe took his men and the immigrants and hid behind the dry river bank.

The lights from the truck came over a hill about a half mile away. The two Border Patrol officers stood by their vehicle, both with weapons drawn but hidden from view, waiting to see who was interrupting their business.

When the truck was about a hundred yards away they could see it wasn't a truck at all, it was a bus, a large yellow school bus. It came to a stop next to the SUV and the door hissed open. The bus appeared empty except for the driver. They watched as the driver walked down the bus steps and said, "Good evening, officers. My name is Joshua and I'm here to pick up the illegal aliens and transport them to Nogales for processing."

Bull looked at Jake with a confused expression and began to speak, but Jake waved him off. He stared at the driver for a few moments before speaking. The driver was a large, very large, black man dressed in body armor with not one, but two, side arms, with a taser and pepper spray also on his belt.

"Who authorized this pick up?" Jake asked, as he eased the safety off on his Glock, still held out of site.

The big man smiled and answered, "It was Jesus. Jesus was the one who authorized it." When Joshua said "Jesus," he said it like the Spanish name (hey soos).

Jake thought for a moment, then said, "I've never heard of a Jesus in the Border Patrol."

"He's new to the Nogales area," replied Joshua.

Jake's gun came up fast but Joshua was faster. He put two bullets in Jake's head before he could fire a shot. Bull had forgotten to release the safety on his weapon and it cost him his life. Joshua shot him twice in the head and watched him fall to the ground.

Joshua walked by the SUV and went down the hill with both weapons drawn. He knew what was coming next. He slipped on his night vision glasses and easily spotted all three coyotes, two with assault rifles, one with a pistol. Before they could fire a shot, he killed them quickly. He returned his weapons to their holsters and took the money off of El Jefe's body.

He spoke in perfect Spanish in a voice loud enough for all to hear. "My name is Joshua. I am here to take you to safety. I have killed the men who were going to rape your women and then kill you all. I have food and water in the bus and I will return the money you paid to the coyote, the pig known as El Jefe. I know you have no reason to trust me, but I will not harm any of you. Please let me take you to safety."

One by one, slowly at first, they all came out of hiding and got on to the bus. The girl who Bull was going to rape was the last one. She alone came up to him and said, *"Muchas gracias, señor, por todo."* She took his hand and together they walked to the bus.

ABOUT THE AUTHOR

I've been a fan of science fiction ever since I was in grade school (a very long time ago). In those days there were three outstanding authors: Isaac Asimov, Arthur C. Clark, and Robert A. Heinlein.

My favorite author was Heinlein. He began writing his science fiction stories for young people. His first books were categorized as 'Boys Books.' Today, they're called 'Young Adults.' His stories were very believable to me and I couldn't wait to get to his latest books. As I matured, so did his books. I have read every book Heinlein published and still have most of them in my personal library. I think my all-time favorite Heinlein story is *Stranger in a Strange Land.*

My current favorite author is Orson Scott Card. Again, like Heinlein's stories, I find myself 'living' the story as it unfolds. *Ender's Game* and *Prentice Alvin* are two of my favorite Card novels.

I've always had an interest in writing science fiction novels. I would read books by new authors and say to myself, "I could write a better story." However, when I tried, publishers didn't agree. When Covid-19 broke out, I had a lot of spare time on my hands and decided to give it another shot.

During the last three years, I have written nine action/adventure, sci-fi novels and hope to finish the manuscript for the forth book in the Joshua series soon. The good Lord willing, I intend to keep them coming.

**If you enjoyed reading *Caleb's Tale*
you'll love the other books in the War on Crime series.**

Joshua recounts the three trial missions he is required to conduct without the aid of Caleb. As he moves from one mission to the next, they become more complicated and deadlier.

The spirit of Caleb teams with his brother in *Caleb and Joshua* in a much more complicated mission; shutting down five major drug cartels. This year's Mardi Gras in New Orleans becomes deadly, very deadly.